Man and baby t[...]

Standing in her drivewa[...] [Tyler] [looked] too gorgeous for her peace of mind. It took two seconds to figure out she wasn't immune to him. She'd been out of action when it came to dating and sex. But right then, in low-riding jeans and a baby on his hip, Tyler was the sexiest man she'd ever seen. And her hibernating libido immediately kick-started out of slumber.

"You wanted me," he said, his blistering gaze connecting with hers. "So you have me."

She could have played dumb, but she knew she'd swindled him out of his hotel and onto her ranch. "So you'll stay?"

"*We'll* stay. For a week."

Part of her was delighted but another part was nervous. After two years, sharing her home with a man tied her belly in knots.

This is about the baby... not him.

She took a deep breath and led him inside. As he entered, he turned to look at her. A gust of awareness swept the house, an intimacy that defied logic and made her hot all over. His gaze held her captive, and no matter how she tried, she couldn't look away.

It was going to be a long week.

* * *

THE COWGIRL'S
FOREVER FAMILY

BY
HELEN LACEY

First Published in Great Britain 2016
By Mills & Boon, an imprint of HarperCollins*Publishers*
1 London Bridge Street, London, SE1 9GF

© 2016 Helen Lacey

ISBN: 978-0-263-92020-8

23-0916

Our policy is to use papers that are natural, renewable and recyclable products and made from wood grown in sustainable forests. The logging and manufacturing processes conform to the legal environmental regulations of the country of origin.

Printed and bound in Spain
by CPI, Barcelona

Helen Lacey grew up reading *Black Beauty* and *Little House on the Prairie*. These childhood classics inspired her to write her first book when she was seven, a story about a girl and her horse. She loves writing for Mills & Boon Cherish, where she can create strong heroes with a soft heart and heroines with gumption who get their happily-ever-after. For more about Helen, visit her website, www.helenlacey.com.

For my wonderfully supportive editor,
Susan Litman— who allowed me the time
I needed for this one. Thank you.

Chapter One

Brooke Laughton shot up in bed.

Rubbing her eyes, she quickly checked the clock. Nine twenty. She'd been in bed for less than fifteen minutes. The dogs were barking, which meant either one of the horses were out, a feral cat had found its way into the chicken run again—or someone was skulking around the ranch house.

Swinging her legs off the bed, she pulled on the sweatpants she'd discarded fifteen minutes earlier and grabbed her sweater. The dogs were still barking and she heard a sound—the slam of a car door. Tension snaked up her spine. Not that she was scared. She could handle herself *and* the rifle she kept stashed in her wardrobe. She grabbed the gun, shoved her feet into a pair of loafers and left the room. The floorboards creaked as she made her way down the hallway and when she reached the living room doorway, she blinked at the lights beaming through the front window.

Headlights.

Brooke went to the front door and placed the rifle by the jamb. She had a security screen and since the dogs were still going ballistic, she felt safe enough to open the door and see what was going on. A light blanket of snow covered the ground and she quickly whistled to her border collies, Trixie and Renaldo, and both dogs immediately left the car and raced up the porch to stand point on either side of the door.

The sensor light flicked on and she waited. A few seconds later the driver's door opened and a tall figure emerged. No one she knew, she thought, or the dogs would have started whining. Instead they both growled low in the backs of their throats. Waiting for her response. Waiting for her reaction.

A man walked toward the house and stopped at the bottom of the steps. He was tall, broad shouldered and dressed in dark trousers and a long-sleeved white shirt and tie and a long coat. He looked respectable enough. And handsome, if you went for the urban, short hair, clean shaven, city boy look.

Not that she did.

She whistled again for the dogs to stop growling and they silenced quickly. But she didn't open the screen door. He might look respectable and harmless, but you could never be too sure. Maybe he was lost? Some of the road signs *were* hard to see in the dark.

"Can I help you?" she asked.

"That depends. Are your dogs going to attack me?"

Oh, yeah, city boy. New York if she wasn't mistaken. "Not unless I give the command," she replied. "Are you lost?"

"I'm not sure," he said and walked up the steps, ignoring the dogs, who were now whining more than barking. "I'm looking for the Laughton Ranch?"

He wanted the ranch? *Her* ranch. Panic set in. Was he from the bank? It seemed unlikely at this time of night… but who would know how these things worked.

"So, you found it," she said, still keeping the locked door between them.

He nodded, looking slightly relieved. "Is Matthew Laughton around?"

He wanted Matt? Then he wasn't from the bank. This was something else. She wondered what her wayward brother had done. And who was this guy…a cop? Or worse—a Fed? She felt ridiculous even thinking it. Maybe a bounty hunter? He didn't look like that, either. But nothing would be a complete surprise when it came to Matt.

"He's not here."

The man stepped closer and she got a better look at him. He was remarkably handsome and her belly did a silly flip, which she promptly disregarded. Good-looking men were nothing but heartache.

The man's gaze narrowed. "When will he be back?"

Brooke shrugged. "I have no idea. What's this about?"

The man reached inside his pocket and withdrew a small business card. "My name is Tyler Madden and I need to see Matthew Laughton urgently."

The dogs had settled and that was enough to convince Brooke he wasn't a threat, so she opened the screen door slowly, pushed it back on the hinges and took the card. She read the words and her stomach sank.

Tyler Madden. Attorney.

She hated lawyers. And this one appeared no different from the other arrogant, slick, condescending mob who were trying to swindle her and steal her ranch—except he was drop-dead handsome. She took a galvanizing breath and spoke in a stern voice. "I don't know where he is, Mr. Madden. I haven't seen my brother for five years."

It was the truth. In a way. Matt hadn't set foot in Cedar River since their parents' funeral. But he did still text her every week to let her know he was okay. Which she wasn't about to admit to this lawyer. This stranger.

"You're his sister?" He paused, as though accessing some memory. "Brooke Laughton?"

"How do you know my name?"

"It's my job to know all the facts in a case."

A case? Her brother was part of a case? It sounded serious. *Oh, Matt...what have you done now?* A chill coursed over her skin. "Please tell me what this is about. What has Matt done? Is he in trouble?"

"Trouble?" He shook his head. "Not exactly. But I do need to speak with him about something important."

Brooke sighed heavily. Did she continue to have the discussion on her doorstep or invite him inside? "Lawyers hours are usually nine till five. Isn't it a little late for a house call? Can't this wait until the morning?"

He shrugged. "I'm booked into a hotel in town, but when I missed the turnoff I realized I was close to your ranch. And since the issue I need to discuss with your brother is one of high importance, I didn't think the time mattered."

It was a logical explanation. Sort of. "That's easy enough to do," she said. "They rerouted the highway about seven years ago. There's only this place and the bigger ranch next door along this road now." And if she wanted to know more she figured she needed to let him inside. "I suppose you should come in and explain what this is about."

He hesitated for a second and then spoke. "Ah...sure. Just give me a minute."

When he turned around and headed back toward the car Brooke stared after him. Maybe he wasn't so harmless after all? What was he doing in the car? Looking for an axe? A gun?

She glanced at her rifle by the jamb and quickly shook the thought off. Trixie and Renaldo were now by the car, jumping around, seemingly happy that he wasn't a threat. She trusted her dogs' instincts. But as he approached the house again she regarded him incredulously.

Because he was carrying a baby.

A baby...

By the time he got to the porch her disbelief had fired up her temper. "You brought a baby with you? In the middle of the night and in this weather? What kind of parent are you? Of all the stupid—"

"This is not my baby," he said quietly, cutting her off as he walked up the steps, then quickly brushed his shoes off on the mat and came across the threshold.

Brooke stared at the child. It was clearly a baby girl, dressed in an immaculate pink jumpsuit and hood and wrapped in a warm blanket, and she was sleeping peacefully against his shoulder. She looked about a year old, not that Brooke had any experience with infants.

Nor will I...

She pushed the thought from her head. Now wasn't the time to reminisce about what she would never have. *Could* never have.

"Then whose..."

"Can I put her down somewhere?" he asked, ignoring her question. "Perhaps the sofa?"

Brooke nodded and closed the door. "Of course. This way."

He motioned to the rifle by the door. "Was that intended for me?"

"If you were a threat…then, yes."

"I'm not a threat to you," he assured her.

"I guess I decide that once you tell me what this is about."

She led the way to the living room and pointed to the big chintz sofa. He gently set the sleeping child down and secured a couple of cushions around her. Once he was done he straightened and let out a short sigh.

"This is about Cara," he said, looking at the baby and then back to Brooke. "And she's your niece."

The breath rushed from her throat and she glared at him. "My what?"

Tyler hadn't intended to show up on Brooke Laughton's doorstep in the middle of the night. But he was all out of patience by the time he realized he'd missed the turnoff for Cedar River and since he was so close to where he needed to be, he took his chances. The long flight from New York, the mix-up with the rental car and a screwy GPS had done nothing to improve his mood. And Cara had been unusually restless most of the trip. He really should have brought the nanny with him to look after her. But he was all out of patience with that idea, too. He hadn't liked the woman and her bossy ways. She was more drill sergeant than nanny. It was better this way and meant one less complication to deal with.

He was in Cedar River, South Dakota, to fulfil a promise he'd made to a dying girl and to an old man to whom he owed an enduring debt. He'd promised Ralph Jürgens that he would try and place Cara with her biological father, and that's what he would endeavor to do.

Tyler looked at the woman standing barely three feet from him. She was pretty in a hometown kind of way. Her thick blond hair was tied up in a messy ponytail and she had freckles across the bridge of her nose. She had nice features and clear skin and although the sweats she wore were shapeless, he was sure there were curves underneath. But it was her eyes that caught his attention. Indigo eyes. So blue they appeared violet. The baby had the same color eyes. If he'd had any doubts that twelve month old Cara was Matt Laughton's child they quickly disappeared.

"Your brother's child."

She gasped. "I don't believe it. Matt wouldn't be so—"

"Irresponsible?" Tyler finished for her. He knew enough about Matthew Laughton to figure that being *responsible* wasn't on his radar. "Now, we both know that's not true."

Her chin hiked up. She had a temper, that was for sure. He wasn't sure why it intrigued him, but it did.

"If Matt had a child he would have told me."

"He doesn't know about the child," Tyler explained. "Which is why I am here. If you can give me a number where I can reach him we should be able to sort this out quickly."

She didn't look like she was prepared to give him anything. Except perhaps a punch in the nose. It only took a few minutes in her company to realize that Brooke Laughton wasn't about to simply comply with his demands and give him Matthew's contact details. She wanted answers. And her next words confirmed that.

"Not until you explain the situation to me fully, Mr. Madden."

Tyler sighed heavily and motioned to the other sofa. "Shall we sit?"

She eyed him warily, but nodded and plonked herself on the single love seat by the fireplace. Tyler sat on the sofa, rested his elbows on his knees and looked around the room. There was a large family portrait above the fireplace and she looked to be around fifteen in the photograph. There were other pictures on the mantel—an old couple he assumed were her grandparents, and another of Brooke with three other women all wearing evening gowns and holding up champagne flutes. Family and friends—they were clearly important to her. A few Christmas cards sat on the mantel but there was no tree or gifts in the room.

Christmas. It was barely a week away. And not his scene. Maybe it wasn't Brooke Laughton's, either. Regardless, with any luck he'd be back in New York before the week was out.

"So?" she asked. "I'd like an explanation."

Tyler nodded and focused his attention on the woman in front of him. "A little under two years ago your brother had a brief relationship with a young woman called Yelena Jürgens. That relationship resulted in Yelena's pregnancy. By the time she discovered she was pregnant Matthew was long gone and she chose not to tell him about the baby."

Her gaze narrowed. "Why not?"

Tyler shrugged lightly. "I'm not privy to what went on in their relationship. He was gone by then and Yelena was alone. I do know that Yelena wanted the child and planned to care for the baby herself."

Brooke Laughton was quiet for a moment, looking at him and then the sleeping child. "And where is Yelena now?"

"She passed away four months ago," Tyler explained. "She had kidney failure brought upon by diabetes that she'd suffered with all her life. She was scheduled for a transplant but wouldn't accept treatment or surgery once she knew she was pregnant."

He watched as she swallowed hard and he saw a shadow of sadness in her expression. "And so where do you fit into this little story?"

"I'm her grandfather's lawyer. And friend," he added quietly. "I've known Ralph Jürgens for eighteen years. Ralph is Yelena's grandfather and her only relative. Her parents were killed many years ago and Ralph raised her."

"That's so sad. But...this baby...are you sure she's my brother's—"

"Positive," he said, cutting her off. He withdrew an envelope from the pocket inside his jacket and passed it to her.

"What's this?" she asked and opened the letter.

"Cara's birth certificate," he explained. "As you can see, your brother is named as the child's father."

"But that could just be—"

"I met your brother several times when he was involved with Yelena," he said, cutting through her protest. "And they certainly appeared to have had an intimate relationship."

She looked shocked. Disbelieving. Cynical. "If Matt knew about the baby he—"

"But he didn't," Tyler interrupted. "As I explained, Yelena discovered she was pregnant *after* your brother left New York. It was only at the end of her illness that she instructed me to find him and tell him he was Cara's father. Paternity can certainly be confirmed with DNA testing if needed."

Her gaze narrowed. "You said she died four months ago."

"Yes," he replied. "When Cara was nearly eight months old."

"And it's taken you that long to track Matt to here?"

Tyler half shrugged. "Not exactly. When Yelena died

her grandfather asked me to hold off contacting your brother. Ralph had hoped he would be able to take on the responsibility himself."

"But?"

"He's eighty-five and knows he hasn't got too many years left," Tyler said flatly, ignoring the way the words echoed deep down in his chest. "He's too old and frail to care for Cara himself."

"And there are no other relatives?" she asked, now perched on the edge of the seat.

"No. Just your brother," he replied.

She gasped a little, like she couldn't get enough air in her lungs. He watched her, intrigued by the resolve she was showing. Brooke Laughton had gumption and backbone—that was clear. And strength. Something he knew Matt Laughton was severely lacking. But despite her grandfather's protests, Yelena had insisted Matthew be told about the baby.

"Can I...can I see her?" she asked with uncertainty.

"Of course," he said and stood.

He got up, took a couple of steps and gently flipped back the blanket covering the baby. Cara stirred a little, but then relaxed and moved her tiny mouth in the way he'd become so accustomed to. Over the past few months Ralph had employed one nanny after the other and when that hadn't worked, Tyler had taken over and hired the drill sergeant. But he made sure he saw Cara every day, just to ensure she was being cared for correctly.

"She's so beautiful," Brooke Laughton said with a sigh.

Yeah...women and babies...it never failed to be one of the wonders of the world.

He knew she was thirty-two, never married and without children. She looked very much like an independent, spirited woman who could look after herself. And yet, there was a softness in her expression as she gazed upon her sleeping niece.

"Yes, she is," Tyler said quietly. "Like all babies, I imagine."

She glanced at him. "Do you have any?"

"Kids?" He shook his head. "No."

"Me, either," she said softly. "Is she okay... I mean, healthy?"

"Perfectly," he replied. "She eats well and is generally a happy baby."

Her brows rose. "You've spent a lot of time with her?"

"Since Yelena died? Yes, I have. I had a nanny looking after her at the Jürgenses' Manhattan apartment but I have tried to see her every day. Ralph is old and not in good health, as I said."

"Does he agree with your decision to bring her here?"

"He does now," Tyler replied. "Yelena wanted her daughter to be raised by family. And that family is now your brother."

And me...

Brooke's heart was pounding so hard she was sure the man beside her could hear it.

Cara's peaceful expression tugged at her, deep down. *Her niece. Her family.* It seemed like someone had just handed her the moon.

And that someone took the shape of the tall and handsome man now standing barely a foot away from her. He had green eyes, she noticed. And his hair was like the color of Beechwood honey. He had the kind of broadshouldered, long-limbed build that had always attracted her. Still, he *was* a bit of a pretty boy. There was noth-

ing weathered about his face. Nothing other than perfect
symmetry and a strong jawline.

She looked at the baby again and something uncurled
inside Brooke, a kind of deep yearning that took root way
down in her womb. "How old is she?"

"Eleven months and three weeks," he replied. "She'll
turn one at the end of next week. She was born on Christmas day."

What a wonderful gift, Brooke thought. "Is she walking?"

"Wobbling," he said, grinning fractionally, and a dimple appeared in his cheek.

Damn…she'd always been a sucker for dimples. "She
looks so peaceful," she said, quickly ignoring him, his
green eyes and his dimples.

"Say that when she wakes you up at five in the morning."

She sat on the coffee table and took a deep breath.
Cara's hands rested against the edge of the blanket and
Brooke reached out to stroke her thumb. The baby moved
and then sighed and her fingers softly curled around
Brooke's. A feeling unlike any she'd known before uncurled in her chest. This child was her blood. And in that
moment she knew she would do whatever she had to, to
make sure Cara was raised on the ranch that had been in
the Laughton family for five generations.

Which meant she had to contact her brother. And fast.

"Thank you for bringing her here, Mr. Madden. Cara
will be well cared for, I assure you."

"It's my job to see that she is," he said quietly and took
a seat beside the sleeping child.

Brooke realized that their knees were almost touching. She also realized it was the closest she'd been to a
man for over two years. Since Doyle had left. Or since

he'd traded her for a woman who could give him what she couldn't. She pushed past the sudden surge of emptiness in her heart. For the moment she had only one priority, and that was her niece.

"Where is he?"

Brooke lifted her gaze and met Tyler Madden's inquiring stare. "Matt?" She shook her head. "I told you, I don't know where he is."

"So, you've had no contact with him for five years?"

"I didn't say that," she replied. "I haven't seen him for five years. But he sends me a message each week."

"In what form?" he asked, his gaze narrowing. "Email? Smoke signal?"

He really was a lawyer, she thought irritably. He was as condescending as they came. Brooke got to her feet and moved back to the chair. "Text message."

"You have his phone number?"

"I have *a* number," she said. "Whenever I've tried to call, it always goes to a voice mail. I'm sure it's just a burner cell he keeps to let me know he's okay."

"Can you call the number now?"

"And say what?" She shot back. "'Hey, Matt, you'd better get your butt back home pronto because you're a daddy'?"

"That should do it."

Brooke's patience frayed. "Look, Mr. Madden, I know you—"

"Tyler."

"What?"

"That's my name."

Brooke glared at him. He really was annoying. "I think we should keep this professional."

He laughed softly. "You're not my client, *Brooke*," he said and tucked the blanket back around the baby.

"Neither is your brother. Ralph Jürgens is my client, and Cara's welfare is my priority. So, now we have that settled, I would appreciate it if you would make the call to Matthew."

Brooke got to her feet. There was no point being stubborn and antagonizing him. "Okay. I'll make a call."

She left the room and got to the kitchen in double quick time. Then she came to an abrupt halt and gripped the back of a chair for support. There was a man and a baby in her house! It was enough to make her hyperventilate. Brooke grabbed her phone off the big scrubbed table and flicked through to her messages. Matt had left his last message four days ago.

Hi. All good here. Speak soon. M

It was as vague as any he'd sent over the years. Brooke dialed the number and waited for the familiar peal of an unanswered call. She left a message asking him to call her back, and then tucked the phone into her pocket and walked back into the living room. And stopped in her tracks.

Tyler Madden was sitting on the sofa and Cara was cradled in his arms. Brooke swallowed hard. Her belly and her heart were foolishly doing somersaults. This man was a stranger. And worse…a *lawyer*. He had a job to do, that's all. Thinking he looked too sexy for words was just plain old stupid. And she wasn't a stupid woman. She'd stopped being stupid the day her ex had sprinted out the door.

"You look like you've had practice doing that," she said and stepped into the room.

He met her gaze. "I've had some experience. She was restless for a moment."

Brooke came around the sofa. "Do you come from a big family?"

He ignored her question. "Did you reach your brother?"

"I left a message asking him to call me. I'll try again in the morning."

"Thank you," he said and stood, holding the baby close to his chest. "I should get going. I'll call you tomorrow to find out if your brother has contacted you."

"Where are you staying tonight?"

"I have a room at a place called O'Sullivans."

She nodded as a kind of unease settled in her belly. "It's the big hotel in town. It's nice... I'm sure you'll be comfortable there. Are you..."

His green-eyed gaze narrowed. "Am I, what?"

Brooke straightened her shoulders. "Are you taking Cara with you?"

"Of course," he replied and took a step away from the sofa. "I'm her legal guardian."

Brooke's unease slowly turned into a rising panic. Her guardian? Which meant he was calling all the shots. "So, that means you get to decide what happens to her."

"It means I get to decide if your brother is a fit and able parent...assuming he returns your call, gets himself back to Cedar River and actually wants to be Cara's father."

Her stomach sank. *Oh, Matt...please call back.*

"And if he doesn't?"

Tyler Madden glanced down at the baby before he returned to her unsteady gaze. "Then it is my responsibility to find Cara a suitable home."

"A suitable home?" Brooke echoed, her apprehension growing. "What does that mean?"

"What does it usually mean?" he said. "A home. A family."

"You mean, she'll be adopted?"

"Exactly."

His reply made her blood run cold. Adopted out to strangers? "She's my brother's child and therefore *my* family and I have a right to—"

"This isn't about your rights," he said quietly. "This is about doing what is best for Cara. Hopefully, and in accordance to Yelena's wishes, that is your brother. You need to understand that Ralph has reservations about Matt being a fit parent for Cara. But, he's willing to do what Yelena wanted if your brother can prove that he is willing to be a father. If he's not, or if he's unable to be found, then I'll consider other options."

Other options? *That's here, where she belongs...*

But Brooke held her tongue. First, she had to get her brother back to Cedar River. Which wasn't going to be easy. Second, she had to convince Matt that he had to act like a responsible adult and be a parent to the child he'd fathered. That wasn't going to be easy, either. Matt had been on the run for five years. Since the accident that had killed their parents. He still blamed himself, even though another driver was at fault. Nothing she said eased his grief, his guilt or managed to convince him it was time to come home. But maybe this would, she thought as she gazed at the sleeping child. All she had to do was convince Tyler Madden to give her some time.

Which meant being friendly. Or at least civil.

"I understand you have a job to do and I appreciate that Cara's welfare is important to you, but please understand that as her aunt and her family, it's important to me, too. Even if I didn't know she existed until about half an hour ago, I'm trying to get past the shock and concentrate on doing what's best for her."

He stood rigid, looking unmoved by her impassioned

speech. She wouldn't have expected anything else. He was a lawyer doing his job. He had no emotional investment, only duty. She knew enough about lawyers to recognize one that was as cold as a fish.

"Get in contact with your brother," he said and pulled his car keys from his pocket. "And we'll see what happens from there."

Brooke was tempted to snatch the baby from his arms, but quickly ditched that idea. He was big and strong and, despite the civilized suit and tie, she suspected he could handle himself in the courtroom, the bedroom or a street brawl if he needed to, let alone in a tussle with a woman who was barely five feet five inches tall.

She fingered the business card in her hand. "I'll contact you as soon as I hear from Matt."

He nodded. "Thank you. Good night."

Brooke followed him down the hall and watched as he walked through the front door and then down the steps. The dogs sat at heel by the door and she waited while he secured the baby into the backseat of his sedan and drove off, staring at the disappearing taillights. Once she saw the car turn off on the main road Brooke shut the door, took a long breath and pulled the cell phone from her pocket. She dialed Matt's number again and left another message—this one more urgent than the last.

He had to come home. And until he did, Brooke would do whatever she could to ensure Cara stayed in town. Which meant she'd play whatever game Tyler Madden had planned.

For now.

Chapter Two

A distraction. That's what she was. That's *all* she was. And Tyler didn't want or need any distractions. But damn if he didn't spend the night dreaming about indigo eyes and freckles.

He was in Cedar River for business—that was all. He had a job to do and a child to care for…so dreaming about Brooke Laughton was off-limits.

The O'Sullivan's hotel was surprisingly well-appointed and much more opulent than he'd expected. The night duty manager had quickly sourced a crib for the baby, so Tyler didn't have to lug out the portable one he'd stashed in the trunk of the rental car, which was great since the weather had turned worse and the snow was coming down heavier. He didn't sleep much but was pleased that Cara had slept soundly and awoke in a happy mood. He bathed and changed her and ordered coffee from room service. Once she'd eaten some cereal and had a bottle he placed her back in the crib and took a shower. When he was done he changed into dark chinos and a blue shirt and opened up his laptop.

He'd taken a couple of weeks' leave from Wall, Hardin & Steele, but he still had two open cases that needed his attention. He'd been with the firm for five years and was up for partner in the next six months. It's what he wanted. What he'd worked for.

Phil Hardin hadn't been happy that he had asked for time off to sort out Cara's situation, but Tyler had insisted. He owed Ralph Jürgens his time and attention.

What I want...what I've worked for.

He had to keep remembering that. Nothing was going to distract him.

It was just after ten when the room phone rang. He snatched it up and the clerk at reception informed him that he had a visitor. His stomach immediately tied itself in knots.

Indigo eyes...

He cursed to himself for thinking like a fool but when he opened the door to her a few minutes later, his awareness level almost shot into the red zone. She looked incredible in a bright green, long-sleeved collared T-shirt tucked into the waistband, a sheepskin vest, a wide leather belt and cowboy boots. Well-worn jeans that accentuated her long legs clung to the curves of her hips, and her golden hair hung down over her shoulders. No makeup—just the healthy glow of someone who worked outdoors.

Damn...she stirred him. More than he'd been stirred in a long time. Since...forever.

"Hi," she said, kind of breathlessly.

"Hi, yourself."

"I was in town," she explained quickly. "Getting horse

feed and some fencing gear. So I thought I'd drop by and see Cara. Is that okay?"

Tyler shrugged one shoulder. "Sure. Come on in."

She walked into the room and the scent of her perfume fluttered through the air. Or maybe it was simply her shampoo. She didn't strike him as a woman who spent time preening and powdering. There was something effortlessly earthy and natural about her and it had an unexpected effect on him. He knew prettier women. Dated and slept with them whenever the mood took him. But he always kept it casual. No commitment, no deep feelings. Sex and company. That was his mantra. Once the need started he bailed. Because of that he generally dated a certain kind of woman—someone with the same outlook he had. Someone who lived to work and didn't expect too much of his time and attention. It was superficial, shallow and exactly what he wanted. Exactly what suited him. One day, he figured he'd settle down. He wanted a family of his own at some point. He'd find the right woman and get married and have a couple of kids with someone who understood him. And small town girls with big eyes, sweet smiles and freckles were not part of that agenda.

Not ever.

He watched as Brooke headed straight for the crib. She hung back at first, almost hesitating, until Cara responded and held out her chubby arms and then Brooke gently lifted her up. He watched silently, witnessing the bond that was becoming evident. Blood ties. He'd never felt it. Never known it.

But blood and family were obviously important to Brooke.

"Have you heard from your brother?" he asked and closed the door.

She looked across the room and the smile she'd given

Cara faded slightly. "Not yet. I sent another message this morning. He'll call... I'm sure of it. And once he knows about this darling girl I know he'll come back."

Tyler wasn't so sure. Oh, he knew Cara *should* bring Matthew back home. But Matt Laughton didn't strike him as a young man who was swayed by what he *should* do. However, he'd made a commitment to Yelena to give the other man a chance to do what was right. And he would. For the moment.

"I hope you're right," he said quietly and watched as Brooke cradled the baby on her hip and began talking to her.

After a moment, as though aware she was being observed, she met his gaze. "She's so beautiful. Her eyes are—"

"Like yours," Tyler said quietly. "The same color."

She nodded, like it pleased her. "She looks like Matt did when he was a baby. My mom said he was way too pretty to be a little boy," she said and laughed softly. "I always liked to tease him about that when we were growing up."

"You were close?"

She shrugged a little. "I guess. I'm eight years older than him so I was very much the big sister. But yeah, we were close... I mean...until he left when our...when..."

"When your parents were killed?"

Her eyes darkened. "Yeah...then."

He knew her parents had been dead for five years. Knew Matthew had been driving the car that afternoon. But he was interested in knowing the details. "Would you tell me what happened?"

She sat down on the small couch and held Cara in her arms. The baby gurgled and laughed and Brooke's expression was one of pure delight. Something uncurled in his chest, a strange sensation that was rooted deep down. He'd never been sentimental or allowed himself to get close to anyone and he couldn't explain what he was feeling. Nor did he want to.

After a moment she looked up. "I'm pretty sure you already know."

"I know what the case file says," he replied. "I know Matthew was driving the car and that he crashed and your parents were killed instantly."

"Then you know everything."

"Really?"

She shrugged again, harder this time. "He *was* driving, but the accident was not his fault. There was another driver who—"

"I don't recall another driver being mentioned in the file I read."

"No," she said and grimaced. "You won't. The driver fled the scene."

"And no charges were ever filed?"

Brooke rocked the baby gently and met his gaze for just a moment. "It's complicated. And really none of your concern."

"If it's the reason why your brother is reluctant to return home then it is my concern."

"Matthew doesn't come home because he feels guilty," she said, hostility flashing in her eyes. "Our parents were killed. So was Sky Dancer. Matt couldn't get past the—"

"Sky Dancer?" Tyler queried, remembering the file had mentioned something about a horse being killed in the crash. "That's the horse that was killed?"

"He wasn't just a horse. He was our foundation stallion," she explained. "The ranch used to be renowned across the state for its quarter horses. Sky Dancer was the stallion that my father built that breeding program on. Without my father and Sky Dancer the ranch stopped being a working horse ranch and instead…"

"Instead?" he prompted.

She sighed. "Instead it became a place where I give trail rides to tourists in summer and run a few dozen head of cattle to try and keep the place solvent."

Her voice held all the disappointment of dreams lost and something unexpected uncurled in his chest.

Tyler didn't do sympathy. His job taught him to be impartial and detached. But Brooke Laughton's haunted indigo eyes were hard to stay out of. "And do you want to return it to what it once was?"

She sighed again and rocked the now chattering baby on her knee. "Of course. One day I'll buy Cloud Dancer and I'll be able to—"

"Cloud Dancer?" he inquired, one brow raised.

"Sky Dancer's grandson," she replied. "He's on the show circuit at the moment but lives on a ranch in Montana. He's every bit the horse his grandfather was…same strong lines, same unflappable temperament. When I was competing I rode him several times and he always gave his all."

Tyler was uncharacteristically mesmerized by the passion in her voice. Her cheeks were flushed and her eyes shone brightly, like he'd struck a nerve with the mention of horses. He vaguely remembered Yelena telling him that Brooke used to be a professional barrel racer and how Matthew had been in awe of her commitment and success on the show circuit. It fascinated him. "Your horses mean a lot to you?"

Her gaze narrowed, like she was immediately looking for the insult in his words. "Do you think that's nuts? Maybe it is…but I've always felt more at home with animals than I have with most people."

"I would have pegged you for a people person."

"Why?" she laughed. "Because I'm so easygoing?"

Tyler grinned fractionally. "I wouldn't say that exactly. You did have your rifle at the ready last night."

"Can't be too careful these days."

"I guess not. But like I said, I'm not a threat to you."

"I know that," she said and looked at the baby and smiled. "Besides, my dogs are a good judge of character and they liked you. You seem very... I don't know. Civilized."

Tyler laughed softly. Had anyone ever called him that before? Probably not. Not in his personal life and certainly not in the courtroom. Arrogant, cold and detached—that's what he was renowned for. Someone who got the job done without getting bogged down in sentiment. Corporate cases were his specialty and he had a 95 percent win rate. He'd toppled big corporations and wiped out smaller contenders. He worked at one of the top legal firms in New York on a six-figure retainer, owned a penthouse apartment in Manhattan, drove a top-of-the-range BMW and had his suits and shoes made in Italy.

It was quite a leap from being a one-day-old baby dumped in a box and left on a church doorstep in Nowhere, Nebraska.

He ignored the twitch in his gut. Thinking about his beginnings, about the mother who'd abandoned him and then his caring, but tree-hugging, adoptive parents, served no purpose. The past needed to stay where it was. The present was all that mattered.

"Your brother has a week," he said quietly, purposefully, and with every effort to get her eyes and freckles out of his thoughts.

She stared at him. "I know he'll come back. But if he doesn't I assure you that I can look after—"

"If he doesn't come back," Tyler said, cutting her off before she had a chance to plead her case. "Then I'll return to New York with Cara."

"So she can be adopted by strangers?" Brooke shot back. "When she has family right here? When I'm right here?" She took a deep breath. "*I'm* her family. And I have an aunt and cousins and second cousins in this town. I was born here and I've lived here for most of my life. It's a good town with good people. She belongs here. Surely you can see that?"

Tyler knew this was coming. And he admired her desire to make things right. But good intentions weren't enough to raise a child. "You're a single woman and you've just admitted your ranch is in financial trouble. Do you think it's fair to add a child to that struggle?"

Her chin came up. "Plenty of children are successfully raised by single parents. And money isn't the answer to everything."

"No," he said agreeably. "But money is a necessity when raising a child."

He watched as Brooke's clearly rising temper was quickly subdued by the baby's antics. Cara had a way of doing that, he thought and an unexpected wave of affection coursed through him. It was impossible to *not* be attached to the child. She was sweet natured and happy and he'd spent a good deal of time with her over the past few months. Which is why he had to be sure that Matthew Laughton was up to being a parent—if he ever showed his face. As for Brooke, he suspected she'd agree to look after Cara in a heartbeat, but he wasn't going to be swayed from his duty simply because he was unexpectedly attracted to her, especially if she had financial troubles.

"Love is all that matters," she said, scorching him with a hot, resentful glare for a brief second before she quickly got her control back. "And she would get plenty of that right here in Cedar River."

She was naive if she truly believed that, and although Tyler was suddenly all out of patience, he maintained a civil expression. "Well, if your brother fails to show and you can prove that you are able to financially support a child, I will certainly consider your request."

"Thank you," she said and slid onto the floor with the baby to allow Cara to crawl on the carpet. "I appreciate that. I know this must be a difficult situation for you and I understand that you need to put Cara's needs first. So, I was thinking...perhaps you would consider staying at the ranch while we wait for Matthew to come home. That way, when he calls, you can speak to him right away. And... I'd really like to spend some time with Cara."

It wasn't a good idea. In fact, he was sure it was the worst idea possible. He had no intention of living under the same roof as Brooke Laughton...not even for one night.

"No."

Her jaw tightened. But she didn't respond with a temper like he assumed she wanted to. She was appeasing him. Keeping him sweet. Playing him. He suspected she would say and do whatever she thought he wanted to hear. But the lawyer in him was immediately on point.

"No?" she queried. "But you can't really believe a hotel is the best place for a baby."

"I think I know what's best for Cara. And this is very comfortable," he said and waved a vague hand. "Cara has everything she needs and I prefer to be here and not stuck..." His words trailed for a second. "And not so far out of town."

"It's a nice hotel," she said in quiet agreement, clearly holding her tongue. "But it's a *hotel*...not a home. Don't you think she's been through enough already with losing her mom and then traveling across the country to meet strangers? A real home, where she can have a routine and not be surrounded by staff and tourists, makes much more sense. And I'm a pretty good cook, so you could have home-cooked meals every day. Plus, it's Christmas next week."

It was a damned good argument and he admired her approach. But he wasn't going to be swayed. "Good try. You'd make a fine attorney."

Her eyes flashed. There was that temper, he thought. It made him smile a little.

"Please...just say you'll think about the offer. We don't need to be at war over this."

Oh, yeah...she was good.

"I'll take it under advisement," he said and raised a brow.

She opened her mouth to speak and then clamped her lips together tightly. She had a long fuse. And she was smart. He liked that about her. It meant she wasn't a pushover. It didn't mean he was going to move in with her. No way in hell.

By the time she left the hotel room Brooke was so mad she could have punched someone. Or more specifically, knocked Tyler Madden's perfectly straight white teeth down his perfectly gorgeous throat.

She stomped out the elevator and almost collided with the hotel's owner, Liam O'Sullivan. He was another man who thought way too much of himself and his opinions.

"Everything okay, Brooke?" he asked, eyes narrowed.

"Sure. Have you seen Kayla?"

Kayla Rickard was one of her closest friends and Brooke was pretty sure she was sleeping with Liam

O'Sullivan. Kayla had been tight-lipped about the whole affair—probably since Liam and his family were about as unpopular in town as they were rich and powerful—and since Kayla's dad absolutely hated Liam's father for reasons that went back three decades and no one ever talked about.

Liam managed to look a little uncomfortable and checked his watch. "No. She's probably at work."

Kayla was curator of the town's historical museum and art gallery, and Brooke remembered that her friend opened the place for a few hours on Saturday mornings. "Okay, thanks."

She said goodbye and left the hotel. When she got to the pavement she shivered. Winter had come with a vengeance. Snow blanketed the sidewalk and she tread carefully as she took a left and walked the fifty or so feet to the museum. The adobe shop front was original, dating from the previous century—the place had once been the first mercantile in town. The historical society had purchased the building and turned it into a museum about fifteen years earlier.

"Hey there," Kayla said when she walked through the front door.

Her friend came around the reception desk and gave her a hug. Kayla was easily the most beautiful woman she'd ever known. Five foot ten with model-perfect proportions and long blond hair that she always wore in a braid. Although Brooke was a couple of years older they'd been friends since they were in middle school and, along with Lucy Monero and Ash McCune, were as close as any friends could be.

"I need to vent," Brooke said and plonked herself into a chair.

Kayla looked around the empty room. "Go ahead, I'm listening."

She was just about to start spilling her tale of woe when the bell above the door dinged and Ash walked in. Petite and curvy, with flaming red hair, she was a cop who worked for the town's police department. Brooke was glad for the reinforcements. Having her friends around her in her time of need hardened her resolve. It took another minute or so before she had a chance to explain what had happened and when she was done, her two friends were staring at her incredulously.

"And this lawyer says the baby is Matt's?" Kayla asked, eyes wide, mouth agape. "For real?"

"For real," Brooke replied. "And she looks exactly like him anyhow."

"And if Matt doesn't come home he'll take the baby back to New York and see she's adopted?" Ash, who was a single mom to an eleven-year-old son, clearly thought that to be an outrageously bad idea.

"Exactly," Brooke replied. "I don't know what to do. I've called Matt half a dozen times since last night...but nothing. I have no idea where he is. I don't even know if he's in the country. And I had no idea he was ever in New York."

Both women knew her brother's history and both hardly looked surprised that he hadn't made contact. But she refused to give up hope. She had to keep having faith in her brother.

"He said he'll stay for a week. I'm not sure that's enough time."

"You should get your own lawyer," Ash suggested. "In case you need to fight for custody."

She had one. Werner Stewart. He'd been little help in

trying to save her ranch and she suspected he'd be even less help dealing with the custody of a child.

Kayla moved behind the desk and perched herself in front of the computer. "What's this lawyer's name?" she asked.

"Tyler Madden."

Just saying his name made her jumpy. He sure didn't look like any lawyer she'd known. Her own attorney was overweight, balding and wore cheap suits. Tyler Madden, with his broad shoulders and handsome face, looked like he'd stepped off the pages of a magazine. And he'd regarded her with such blistering intensity she felt like she could barely draw enough breath into her lungs.

He was a buttoned-up city boy. It was all the more reason to dislike him. And the way he'd looked down his condescending nose at her suggestion he bring Cara to the ranch—like she lived in some backwater shack. Sure, the ranch house was a little run-down, but it was clean and comfortable and she did her best to maintain the place.

This is comfortable. That's what he'd said about the hotel. Like her home wasn't. *Pompous, patronizing, elitist snob*!

"Oh…hell."

"What?" she asked when Kayla spoke. "What is it?"

Her friend looked up, both brows high. "Do you have any idea who this guy is?"

Her stomach sank. "Not a clue."

"Big-time New York corporate lawyer," Kayla said and sighed as she read from the screen. "He works for one of the city's most influential firms and he rarely loses a case. Ice-man, wolf, shark…they're all words that have been used to describe him. He's serious stuff." Her friend smiled a little. "There's a picture here, too. Wow…and he looks like—"

"I know what he looks like," Brooke said, cutting her off. "And that's got nothing to do with the fact that he's a condescending jerk."

Ash moved around the counter to look at the screen. "Oh…my…that's a really handsome face. Does the rest of him look as good?"

"He's a condescending jerk," Brooke said again.

"He's really rubbed you up the wrong way, hasn't he?" Kayla remarked, smiling.

"He hasn't 'rubbed me up' in any way," Brooke said, ignoring the innuendo. "He turned up on my doorstep last night with a baby he says is my niece and demanded to see Matt. This morning all I did was suggest he stay at the ranch while we wait for Matt to make contact and he wouldn't even consider it. I know for Cara's sake I have to be civil, but being nice to him makes me want to smack him over the head with a shovel."

Both women laughed and it made Brooke grin.

"It's been a long time since any man has made you have this kind of reaction," Kayla said. "Or any reaction, come to think of it. Since Doyle."

Brooke huffed out a breath. The last person she wanted to think about was her ex-fiancé. Both women had been there for her when Doyle Sharpe walked out the door. Sprinted out, really. Five years together—three on the show circuit and two back in Cedar River—and she thought they would settle down and make a home together. But it wasn't to be. Doyle wanted something else. Something more. Children. The one thing she could never give him. One surgery after another when she was younger had made that impossible. He'd told her it didn't matter…that he was prepared to forgo children if it meant they could be together. Until Deedee Price, his former girlfriend, showed up in town with a six-year-old son in tow. A child that was his. Doyle had hung around for three days before he packed up his things and followed Deedee to Texas.

"Let's not bring that up. And I haven't had a *reaction* to him. All I want is for this lawyer to realize that as Cara's aunt I have some rights and would like to spend some time with her. All I have to do is get him to agree to come and stay at the ranch."

Kayla frowned. "Are you sure you want him *living* with you?"

"I don't want *him*," she replied hotly. "This is about the baby. She's a Laughton and she belongs at the family ranch. With me, until Matt gets here. After that…well, we'll work it out as we go along. Except Tyler Madden is being stubborn and hateful."

"He's only doing his job," Ash said gently. "You know that, right? I'm sure it's not personal."

Maybe not, but it sure felt personal. "She's my niece," Brooke said. "My family. Not his. She's nothing to him."

"But they clearly come as a package deal," Ash said. "If he's her legal guardian and he won't simply leave her there with you, what can you do? He has the law on his side, and he's a high-powered attorney with a whole lot of resources."

"I'm not about to kidnap her," Brooke reassured her friend. "So you won't have to arrest me anytime soon. I just have to get him to see that living in town in a hotel isn't what's best for Cara. And that living at the ranch with me is."

"So, you need to change his thinking?" Kayla suggested.

"Precisely." Brooke raised her brows toward her friend as an idea formed. "If only I could influence Liam O'Sullivan in some way so that he'd kick Mr. Corporate

Lawyer out…like, say the room has been double booked or something and there are no other rooms available in the hotel all week?"

Kayla grinned. "Liam would never go for that. Unless…"

"Unless?" Brooke prompted.

"Unless he didn't know about it."

Ash shook her head. "I don't think I should be listening to this."

Kayla laughed. "Oh, where's your sense of adventure. It's not illegal…and it would really only be a teeny white lie."

A teeny white lie…

Brooke could live with that

Chapter Three

*D*ouble booked?

Tyler stared at the tall blonde who was standing at his door. She wore a loose-fitting corporate jacket with the name of the hotel on the pocket and had just spent over two minutes explaining about some mix-up involving a conference that had been booked months in advance and the guests were due to check in today, which meant a mess of double bookings—and no free rooms.

She looked vaguely familiar but he was certain they'd never met before. By the time she was done speaking his patience was frayed. Under normal circumstances he would have argued the point, demanded a full refund or asked to speak to the hotel manager. But he'd spent an hour trying to get Cara to take a nap and was incxplicably rattled by Brooke's visit, and hadn't done any one of those things. He was tired, irritable and simply wanted to rest for a while. With everything else he had to deal with, Tyler wasn't about to get strung out about a hotel room.

He grabbed his cell phone and looked up the numbers

of other motels in town. There were two, plus a place called Rusty's and a pub called the Loose Moose that each had a couple of rooms to rent. He called them all. But nothing. Rusty's no longer rented rooms, the Loose Moose was under renovation and the two motels were fully booked. Not one room available.

Right. What now? The next closest town was thirty-odd miles away and he certainly didn't want to be that far from Cedar River if Matthew Laughton decided to turn up.

He looked at Cara's things, all packed up and ready to go, still amazed at how much stuff a baby needed to get through the day, and then headed downstairs. The tall blonde was nowhere to be seen and the clerk at reception seemed confused by the whole double-booking scenario.

"Are you and your daughter leaving us already?"

Tyler was two steps from the reception desk when a man spoke to him. He stopped and turned. A suit. And an important one by the look of things. He was about to explain that Cara was not his daughter, but figured it didn't matter. And the less people who knew about his reason for being in town, the better. The man in front of him didn't wear a hotel jacket, but it didn't take a genius to figure out he was probably the owner or manager.

"I'm sure the pretty blonde with the nice smile and the ill-fitting jacket can explain it to you."

"Blonde?" The man frowned and looked at the clerk behind the desk.

The fifty-something woman shrugged and the suit walked around the desk and talked to the woman at length before he looked back up toward Tyler and then promptly apologized for the mix-up.

And it took about two seconds for Tyler to figure out that he had been royally played.

And he knew by who.

Ms. Indigo Eyes had some serious explaining to do!

Tyler propped Cara on his hip and headed out.

He had his car brought around to the front of the hotel and quickly buckled the baby into her car seat, then drove off in search of a drugstore. He needed a few things for the baby and when he found a shop on the main street he quickly pulled up outside. But when he came back out a female cop was standing by his car.

"Is this your car?" she asked, her gaze flicking from the car to the baby in his arms as she regarded him suspiciously.

"It's a rental."

She had a scowl on her face. "Do you realize you're parked in a loading bay?"

He was? Tyler looked toward the hood and saw that the front of the vehicle was pushing barely a foot in the loading bay. "Really? Looks okay to me."

"It's not. We have laws in this town. Can I see your license and registration, please?"

"It's a rental," Tyler explained impatiently and placed Cara in her car seat. It had stopped snowing by now, but the air was chilly and he didn't want to keep her outside unnecessarily.

"License and registration," she said again, tapping a booted heel. "Or I'll have to get this vehicle towed."

Was she serious? He didn't like his chances of getting another rental car on a Saturday afternoon. Cedar River was either the most uptight town on the map or it had to be a joke. Or a scam. Just like the fake double-booked hotel room. He got a good look at her face and quickly realized he'd seen her before. Just like the blonde at the hotel.

The photo on the mantel.

"You know, Officer, you and your blonde accomplice will need to get better at this kind of subterfuge if you're going to be truly convincing," he said and handed over his license.

"What?"

"There's a picture of you both on Brooke Laughton's mantel. There was another woman in the photograph too…a curly haired brunette. What was her part in this plan?"

"I don't know what you—"

"Tell Indigo Eyes she'll have to do better than that," he quipped.

The officer smiled, caught out and unapologetic. "It's strange, I've known Brooke for twenty years and never realized her eyes were exactly that color."

They were…and they'd been haunting him for twenty-four hours.

"Can I go now, Officer?" he asked.

She half smiled and handed back his license. "Well, we gave it a shot."

"The other hotels?" he asked. "How did she manage that?"

"Her cousin Brant owns the Loose Moose—and he's engaged to the curly haired brunette," she explained. "And she knows the owner of Rusty's. It's a small town… and small town folk stick together."

Yes, they certainly did. "What exactly is she after?"

"You," the officer replied and hooked a thumb toward the back of the car. "And that cute baby. She wants you to stay at the ranch while you're here. It's not such a big ask, is it, Counselor?"

He nodded at her badge. "You know very well that in cases like this the less personal involvement, the better."

"I know that people *aren't* cases," she replied hotly.

"You'd know that, too, if you stopped thinking like a lawyer for a moment and thought like a human being. She's a good person…she's honest and loyal and has a heart as big as this state. Brooke wants to bond with her niece… You'd realize that was a good idea if you could get out of the way of your own ego and stop acting like you're in the courtroom."

It was quite the accusation and he was tempted to ask the redhead exactly what Brooke Laughton had told her. But he didn't. Brooke had friends…allies…people willing to go to bat for her. It was admirable. He looked at the baby happily gurgling in the backseat and saw the same chin as her aunt's. He had to do what was best for Cara…and was beginning to suspect that for the moment, Brooke Laughton was exactly that.

He watched the cop walk away and grinned a little. After getting into the car, he drove back to the hotel and checked out. Then he headed for her ranch.

Brooke was finishing up repairing the chicken run out the back of the stables when she heard a car pull up. She instinctively knew who it would be. Ash and Kayla had both given her a heads-up. She dropped the tools and walked around the building, eager to see Cara again. But not so eager to see Tyler Madden.

Because he'd be as mad as hell with her for starters.

And he had every right, if she were being honest with herself.

She shouldn't have tried to swindle him into coming to the ranch. He was too smart for that kind of underhanded approach. And as much as she appreciated her friends coming to her aid, she suspected she'd made a bad situation worse.

She harrumphed under her breath and squared her

shoulders when she spotted his car parked in her driveway. He was resting against the hood and had the baby
in his arms. Cara was wrapped in a pink coat and blanket
and had a fluffy hat on her head. Her cheeks were bright
and against the backdrop of snow on the ground, the two
of them made an enchanting picture. In jeans, boots and
a dark wool jacket, Tyler Madden looked relaxed and
way too gorgeous for her peace of mind. The dogs were
jumping around, clearly delighted to see him again and
not threatened in the least. Brooke stopped about ten feet
from him and planted her hands on her hips.

"Um...hi there."

He didn't say a word. But he looked at her. Out of his
suit he possessed a kind of innate confidence that un-
nerved her. It took her about two seconds to figure out
she wasn't immune to it. Or to him. She'd been under a
rock for two years, off the grid when it came to men and
dating and sex. But right then, in his low-riding jeans and
with the baby on his hip, Tyler Madden was just about
the sexiest and most attractive man she'd ever seen. And
her hibernating libido was immediately kick-started out
of its slumber.

She knew it was foolish. She didn't know anything
about him. He'd said he didn't have children but he could
certainly be married. Or at the very least have a girlfriend. She glanced at his left hand. It was bare. Still,
plenty of married people didn't wear rings.

"You wanted me," he said, not moving, not doing anything other than keeping his blistering gaze connected
with hers. "So, you have me."

"I don't know what you—"

"You know perfectly well," he said, cutting her off.
"Your friends both gave award-winning performances

today. The cop also gave me an earful of advice and said you wanted me here…so, I'm here."

Brooke's breath caught. "It's about Cara," she said breathlessly, taking the *need* and the *want* out of the conversation. "And my friends—"

"Care about you," he said, cutting her off. "Yes, I can see that they do."

Shame crept up her neck. "I'm sorry. I shouldn't have involved them in this. It's complicated enough without—"

"I'll stay."

Brooke stilled instantly. "You'll stay?"

He nodded. "You went to a lot of trouble to get me here. So, yes. I'll stay. *We'll* stay."

It should have made her day. And part of her was delighted—but another part was nervous. She'd lived alone for two years and the prospect of sharing her home with a man, a stranger, tied her belly in knots.

This is about Cara…not him.

"You're not angry?"

"I'm not angry."

"And you'll stay for a week?" she asked.

He nodded again. "Have you heard from your brother?"

Unease pitted in her chest. "Not yet. But he'll call… I know it."

"I hope you're right."

Ignoring the cynicism in his voice, she stepped forward and held out her arms. Cara reached for her immediately and Tyler passed her over—hesitantly, Brooke could tell. She was such a placid, adorable baby and Brooke's heart melted a little more each time she held her.

"Thank you for agreeing to this," she said to Tyler. "If you want to get your things I'll show you to your room."

He pushed himself off the hood and walked around

the car. He looked as good from the back as he did from the front and her wayward belly immediately did another loop-de-loop. She took a deep breath, ignored the feelings and headed inside.

The ranch house had four bedrooms and she walked down the hall to the room opposite hers. Next door to that was a smaller room, where they could set up the crib. She waited while he came in behind her and dropped a bag at the end of the wide bed. He looked around the walls and at the two glass cabinets filled with trophies and awards.

"Yours?" he asked.

She nodded fractionally. "I used to be a barrel racer," she explained. "My parents had a thing for keeping all my awards."

"They were proud of you," he said and dropped his keys on the bedside table. "Understandably."

She smiled. "I suppose. I thought we could put the baby in the room next door to this. It used to be my mom's sewing room but I cleaned out all of her things and now it's the office. Or we could use Matt's room."

"Next door will be fine," he said and roped the baby bag over his shoulder. "I have a portable crib, a playpen and a stroller in the car."

He followed her to the adjoining room and dropped the baby bag on the desk before he disappeared outside. When he returned he had the crib and stroller and quickly set the crib up in the room.

"Looks like you've had plenty of practice doing that," she remarked.

He stopped what he was doing and looked at her. "I guess so. I've spent a lot of time with Cara over the past few months."

She nodded. "The other night you said you came from a large family."

He finished expanding the crib. "I said that?"

Brooke shrugged. "I think so."

"It was more of an extended family," he said and put sheets and blankets in the crib.

"You're so lucky. I only have an aunt and a couple of cousins in town," she said and sat on the chair in the corner, holding Cara close. "And of course Matt. I would have loved one of those big extended families, though, especially around this time of year. Don't get me wrong, I love my family very much. Although, since my parents were killed and Matt left town, there's only about half a dozen of us when we all get together." She swallowed hard as a surge of loneliness swept through her. Five years on and she still missed her parents and only sibling. "But, Thanksgiving and Christmas time is always filled with lots of laughter and love. But with a big family you must have had a happy childhood?"

He stopped what he was doing and looked at her. There was a sudden gust of awareness in the room, an intimacy that defied logic and made her feel hot all over. His gaze held her captive and for a moment she thought how mesmerizing he would be in the courtroom. No wonder he was such a legal hotshot. That green-eyed stare of his riveted her in the chair. She couldn't look away. She couldn't do anything other than stare back.

"My life isn't up for discussion," he said flatly. "I'm here because of Cara."

Brooke raised her chin. Boy, he might be gorgeous, but he was also incredibly uptight. "You don't need to scold me in your best lawyer voice. I wasn't being nosy. Tell me, or don't... I have no opinion about it either way."

"Good."

"Are you married?"

His brows came up. "Didn't I just say my life wasn't—"

"It's not a discussion," she said, cutting him off. "It's a question. I'm only asking because I thought that if you were married perhaps your wife would—"

"I'm not married," he answered quietly.

She was stupidly relieved and then scolded herself. "Girlfriend?"

"Not at the moment."

No wife. No girlfriend. *Available*. That's what her friends would be chanting. But Brooke was determined to *not* be swayed by a gorgeous face and sexy body. Not after Doyle. She didn't have what it took to hold on to a man long term. And she'd had the broken heart to prove it. But still, she did wonder why he wasn't attached. He looked to be in his mid-thirties; surely he'd been close at some point. Maybe he'd had his heart broken, too? Although, he didn't come across as the sentimental type. And from what Kayla had found out about him, he was top in his field and legendary in the courtroom, which might not leave him a lot of time for relationships.

And I'm not going to think about the fact that he'd probably be legendary in the bedroom, too

"Any more questions?"

She gave herself a mental jab. "I just thought that someone might be missing you while you're here."

"No," he said tersely. "Only…"

His words trailed and she raised both her brows. "Only?"

Tyler took a second and cleared his throat. "Mr. Squiggles."

Brooke bit back a smile. "Who?"

"A cat," he said and waved a disinterested hand. "Yelena's cat. I inherited him when she passed away."

Brooke was amused by the color creeping up his neck.

"Mr. Squiggles? I see. And is he a big fluffy white feline who insists on sleeping at the end of your bed?"

His lips twitched slightly. "Black-and-white. And yes, he's known for liking his comforts."

She grinned. "And where is he now?"

"With a neighbor," he replied. "Who will hopefully want to keep him by the time I return to New York."

"You're not a cat person?"

He shrugged one broad shoulder. "I've never thought much about it. But I'm not home much so pets aren't a good idea."

"You work long hours?"

"I do," he replied and pulled a pair of baby monitors out of a bag. Clearly, he was attempting to close the door on this brief glimpse into his personal life. "I'll set one of these up in here and keep the other in the living room or kitchen." He pointed to a small button on the front. "Just make sure this light is on at all times."

"Okay. Does she sleep through the night?"

"Generally," he replied. "She's had a lot to deal with since Yelena died and was unsettled at first. But the last month or so has been better."

Brooke held Cara close and the baby chatted away, murmuring indecipherable words. "And she's been living with her great-grandfather?"

"Yes," he said. "Ralph hired a nanny to care for her."

"Poor little monkey," Brooke said and smoothed her blond hair. "That's a lot to deal with."

"Yes, she's remarkably resilient."

"She's got you, though," Brooke said and smiled. "You seem to care for her a great deal."

Tyler stiffened a bit. "I care what happens to her, of course. She's my responsibility."

"Until Matt gets here?"

"*If* he gets here," Tyler said quietly. "And he will still have to prove he is capable of being a fit and able parent."

Resentment snaked up her spine, but she held her tongue. She didn't want every discussion to end as an argument over her missing brother. "I'm sure he'll do just fine," she said and stood. "What time does she need dinner?"

He glanced at his watch. "In an hour or so. I should give her a bath."

"Oh, let me do it." She snuggled Cara and looked at him. "I mean, if that's okay with you?"

He hesitated a little. "Have you done it before?"

"Yes," she replied instantly. "My cousin Grady has three young daughters and I've been the babysitter countless times."

He nodded. "Okay…she's all yours."

Brooke met his gaze. "Thank you… I mean, for trusting me. It means a lot."

Brooke discovered that bath time was a lot of fun—even though there was more water on the floor than there was in the tub by the time she'd finished. Cara blew bubbles and splashed water and wailed for a moment when Brooke got a little shampoo in her eyes. It wasn't the first time she'd bathed a baby—like she'd told Tyler, her cousin Grady had three young daughters and she'd been a sitter for them many times. She dressed the baby in the pale pink pajamas Tyler had given her, cleaned up the bathroom and then headed for the kitchen.

Tyler was by the window, staring out over the hills and pasture that made up the ranch. His shoulders were tight, as though he had too much pressing down on them, and she fought the internal battle in her head about feeling sorry for him. He was a lawyer. And lawyers were the enemy. He'd threatened to take Cara back to New York if Matt didn't show up. He was not her ally. He was not her friend. He was not her *anything*.

"We're back."

He turned around and half smiled and it made him look even more handsome—if that were possible. "So I see. Did she behave herself?"

Cara wriggled in Brooke's arms and held her hands out toward him. Traitorous child. She walked across the room and let him take her. "She likes to splash."

"I… I can see that," he said, faltering a little as he held the baby against his chest and then glanced away.

Brooke looked down and stilled instantly. The wet T-shirt clung to her curves, leaving very little to the imagination. She folded her arms, conscious of the sudden heat swirling around the room. Heat that was all about the awareness circling between them.

Cara immediately reached out and grabbed a handful of Tyler's hair. He winced and it made Brooke smile. There was love in the baby's eyes and in that moment Brooke realized how much he meant to Cara. "She adores you."

He met her gaze and extricated his hair from Cara's fingers. "Who wouldn't?"

Brooke laughed loudly. "Modest, too, huh?"

"We've spent a lot of time together, haven't we, kiddo?" he said and rocked her gently. "When Yelena died her grandfather didn't cope well. Ralph is a strong man, but Yelena was all he had."

"Her grandfather raised her?"

He nodded. "Since she was eleven. They were very close."

Brooke grabbed the sweater that was hanging on a hook hear the door and slipped into it, zipping it up. Then she came around the counter and flicked on the coffee machine. "He must trust you a great deal... I mean, to leave Cara in your care. You said you've known him a long time—how did you meet?"

He didn't reply straightaway. But he looked at her with such intensity he made her breathless. He was the secretive sort, she thought. No...private. A lot like herself. Brooke never liked talking about herself or her past. Only her closest friends knew about her health battle as a teenager and the ensuing years of treatment and surgery. Or how her parents' deaths had forced her to abandon her professional career so she could ensure the ranch stayed within the family. Or how Doyle had sprinted out the door once he had the chance to have what she could never give him.

Since then she'd had a lonely couple of years, working the ranch, fighting lawyers and the bank who wanted to foreclose. Some days she felt like she had no one to turn to. No shoulder to lean on, to cry on, no arms to hold her tight or a soft voice to tell her everything would be alright. Loneliness had become her shadow and it had made her wary of getting close to anyone again.

But as she looked at Cara, Brooke knew she did want closeness, and family and love. And knowing her niece needed her gave her a kind of strength and resolve she'd thought she'd lost.

"How did you meet?" she asked again.

"When I was sixteen," he said after a moment and sat down at the table, while Cara wriggled in his arms. "He was my court-appointed lawyer."

Brooke's gaze sharpened. "*Your* lawyer?"

"I had filed for emancipation from my parents," he said, his voice void of any emotion.

She sucked in a breath. "Oh, gosh...why?"

His expression narrowed. "It doesn't matter why."

It did, she thought, imagining all kinds of horrors. "Were they mean to you?"

He offered a cynical grin, like he couldn't believe how inquisitive she was. "No, they were kind people. And good parents. They still are."

"But?"

He sighed heavily, clearly irritated by her questions. "They were a little...unorthodox," he said and stood. "We should get Cara fed and—"

"You don't like talking about yourself, do you?"

"Not particularly," he replied. "Do you?"

"No," she said. "But you have the advantage here. I need to make a good impression for Cara's sake, so that means you get to ask whatever you want. And since we're going to be living together for the next week, it's only natural that I might want to know something about you. Plus, it will be a *long* week if we don't speak to each other, don't you think?"

His mouth curled, like he wanted to smile, but didn't. "Okay, you can ask a couple of questions. What would you like to know?"

Brooke inhaled deeply. "You said earlier you don't have a wife. Have you ever been married?"

"No."

"Close?"

He shook his head. "No."

"Longest relationship and who was she?"

He shook his head again. "Six months. She worked in the DA's office."

"Do you have any siblings?"

"No."

"Why did you divorce your parents?" she asked quickly.

"Emancipate," he corrected. "And it's complicated."

Brooke raised both brows. "I'm still listening."

He sighed. "Like I said, they are kind people, but when I was thirteen they took up residence at a shared living community. It wasn't a life that I wanted for myself."

Brooke's eyes widened. "Like a commune?"

He nodded. "I wanted to go to college. They didn't agree with that decision."

She grabbed a couple of mugs and put them on the counter. "So you ran away and got a lawyer."

"I ran away and ended up in social services."

It sounded like a nightmare and made Brooke even more grateful for her happy childhood. "And that's where you met Yelena's grandfather?"

"Correct."

She glanced at him. "Do you still see your parents?"

"Not much."

"They must miss you, though... I mean, if you're their only child. Family and blood ties are important and—"

"I was adopted," he said, silencing her immediately.

Brooke stared at him, thinking of his complicated up-bringing, and feeling an acute kind of sadness deep down. "Thank you for telling me. How old are you?"

"Thirty-four."

"Any vices I should know about?"

He grinned just a little, showing off his dimple. "Not one."

The air between them thickened. There was a kind of seductive energy surrounding him that was impossible to ignore.

"No one is that perfect," Brooke said, feeling heat smack her cheeks. "Take me for instance. I like sweet white coffee, cold toast and I love sleeping in on Sunday mornings."

He propped Cara on his hip and looked at Brooke so

intently that her knees weakened. Suddenly having him living in her house didn't seem like such a great idea.

Because there was something in the air between them.

Something she hadn't experienced for a long time, *felt* for a long time.

Awareness. Attraction. Chemistry. Heat.

Call it by a dozen different names...but it was really only one thing.

Sex...

And it was everywhere. In the air, crawling over her skin, pumping through her blood.

"I like unsweetened black coffee," he said smoothly, not missing a beat, not dragging his gaze from hers. "I like warm toast. And I only ever stay in bed on a Sunday morning if I have a woman in that bed with me."

Chapter Four

Tyler knew he had to stop doing anything that looked or sounded like flirting with Brooke. It was foolish. But there was a kind of relentless energy between them that couldn't be denied. And their complicated situation aside, he liked being around her. She was attractive and intelligent and she made him smile.

Smile?

Since when had that been important?

"Well," he heard her say and endeavored to get his mind back on track. "I don't imagine you'd have too much trouble filling that order."

His interest increased. She was being provocative and probably didn't even know it. "Is there anything else you've been imagining?"

Her cheeks flushed with color and Tyler bit back a grin. She might be fiery, but underneath that bravado was a woman who embarrassed easily.

"Not a thing," she said quickly and moved around the

counter. "So...coffee? Soda?" She opened the refrigerator. "I have beer if you would prefer—"

"Coffee is fine," he said, cutting her off.

She closed the refrigerator and smiled tightly. "Right... one unsweetened coffee on its way."

Tyler watched, absorbed by the easy way she moved around the kitchen. There was something effortlessly natural about her. Most of the women he knew...*all* of the women he knew, were either focused on their career, their appearance, catching a Wall Street husband or all three. But not Brooke Laughton. She was hometown pretty, and her clean skin and long blond hair were getting harder to ignore the more time he spent with her.

She came around the counter a minute later with two mugs and placed them on the table.

"Can I hold her again?" she asked and held out her hands a little.

Tyler nodded, moving forward to pass the baby into Brooke's arms. He caught her scent and his back straightened automatically. Not perfume, but something else, like air and water and fresh baled hay mixed with something as sweet as jasmine. And it was intoxicating. She settled Cara onto her hip and then looked up and smiled at him, and Tyler was instantly drawn into her gaze. Her smile was suddenly mesmerizing, holding his stare. The temperature in the room seemed to hike up several notches, even though he was sure it was just the heat creeping over his skin.

"Everything okay?" she asked as she sat down.

Tyler shrugged and sat opposite her. "Sure."

"I'll make her dinner. Does she have any food allergies?"

"No," he replied and grinned. "She's very open to

eating pretty much anything and everything you put in front of her."

Brooke laughed and the sound reverberated in his chest. "She's clearly a Laughton. My mom used to say that Matt had hollow legs when he was a kid."

The mention of her brother's name quickly changed the temperature in the room. Tyler certainly didn't want to be at odds with her over her brother...but if the other man didn't show up soon there would be hard decisions to make. Decisions he knew Brooke wouldn't take easily. He looked at her, saw that she was frowning and said what was on his mind.

"Brooke, you know he needs to prove he can take care of Cara."

She nodded and stroked the baby's head. "I know that."

"But first he has to actually get here and connect with her. Otherwise..."

"Otherwise," she said when his words trailed off. "You'll hightail it back to New York and see that she's adopted, right?"

"Right," he replied, conscious of an uneasy tension snaking up his spine. "That's my job."

"Even though she'd be better off with me...with her family?"

The strain between them amplified. "I said I'd take that into consideration. I'll also take into account the fact that Matt will have your support should he return."

Cara started babbling to her aunt and Brooke pretended to understand every word. He had to admit that Brooke had quickly formed a bond with her niece. It should have pleased him. But it didn't. If Matt failed to come home then Brooke's bonding might be fruitless. She wanted Cara, that much was obvious. But he wasn't going to rashly commit to leaving Cara in Cedar River without examining every available option. He'd promised Ralph he'd do what was best for the baby and that's what he would do. Maybe Brooke was the best thing for Cara, but he needed time to make a decision. Knowing that, he wondered if his choice to stay at her ranch was a foolish one for more than the obvious reason that pounded through his blood—that he was attracted to her. And more than that.

He liked her.

"I hope..." Her words trailed and he saw the pain in her expression. "I *know* he'll come back."

Unease twitched between his shoulder blades. "He hasn't returned since the accident, has he?"

"That's right."

"Maybe he needs to be told that running away never solves anything."

Her brows came together. "Didn't you run away from home when you were young?"

He nodded. "Yes. Although I'd prefer to think I was running toward something. A new life," he explained, feeling her disapproval. "I wanted an education and a career. Unfortunately, I wouldn't have gotten that had I stayed in Nebraska."

"But you said your parents are good people."

"They are," he replied, very aware that she had somehow flipped the conversation toward him.

"But they're what...hippies?"

He chuckled. "They're what you'd call non-conformists, I guess. They are part of a shared living community where the residents are all about getting back to nature, meditating, growing their own food, being self-sustainable... that kind of thing."

She met his gaze. "That doesn't sound so bad."

"It's not," he said, sensing her disapproval. "It's just not for everyone."

"Not for you, you mean?" she asked, digging deeper.

"Exactly."

Her mouth twisted a little and she looked at him. "Have you met your birth parents?"

Tyler's gut twitched. He hated questions. He never spoke about his past or his upbringing. But Brooke Laughton wouldn't let up. Tyler intended telling her to mind her own business, but once he met her gaze, he couldn't.

"No," he said quietly. "I haven't. And before you go any further with that, no, I never tried to look for them."

Her mouth twisted a little, like she was giving the idea her total consideration. "I think I'd *have* to know…or at least try to find out why they gave me up."

She was unashamedly candid and it was both refreshing and—disconcerting. He never talked about his past. Only Ralph knew the whole story. "I was left on a church doorstep when I was a day old, without a note or explanation," he said and shrugged loosely. "So, I'm pretty sure that means they don't want to be found."

Her eyes widened. "Oh… I'm sorry… I didn't mean to pry and—"

"Sure you did," he quipped. "You're one of those naturally nosy people, right?"

She laughed and the sound echoed around the room. Her eyes were brighter than usual and her cheeks were spotted with color and suddenly he was inexplicably drawn even further into her vortex. There was no other way to describe it. He couldn't remember the last time a woman had had such a profound effect on him. Maybe never. And right then all he could think was how much he wanted to kiss her.

Idiot.

Tyler knew he had to get his head on straight. Kissing Brooke Laughton—even *thinking* about kissing her!—was out of the question. He had one thing to do. To make sure Cara was settled with her father. Or take the baby back to New York if it didn't work out.

Not this.

"I've always thought I was something of a private person," she said and grinned.

Tyler shrugged. "Doesn't mean you can't have an inquisitive streak, too."

"I suppose. Although I'm sure my friends think I'm something of a hermit and spend way too much time alone."

He looked at the baby in her arms, again thinking how naturally she'd taken to being around Cara. "And do you?" he asked quietly.

"Do I spend time alone?" She shrugged. "I suppose I do. The last couple of years have been challenging. After my parents died I moved back here so I could run this place. But then Doyle left and I—"

"Doyle?" Tyler's back straightened instantly.

"My ex-fiancé," she explained flatly, like she had no emotion about it one way or another.

But Tyler wasn't fooled. There was a hollowness in her gaze that spoke volumes. "What happened?"

"We broke up," she replied.

He dug a little deeper. "Was it a mutual breakup?"

She shrugged a little. "Not exactly. Although I can't say I'm unhappy about it now."

"He walked out?"

"More like sprinted out," she said and gave a brittle laugh.

"Why?" he asked quietly, sensing her pain and somehow feeling it through to his blood and bones.

She sighed heavily. "An ex-girlfriend arrived in town with a six-year-old in tow who had eyes just like Doyle's. His son," she said flatly.

"And he left to be with them?" Tyler asked.

"Yes," she replied. "After initially telling me nothing had changed, of course. But three days later he was on his way to Texas."

"Then he wasn't worth having, right?"

"I guess not," she said and pressed a kiss to Cara's forehead. "Anyway, that's all ancient history. Right now, all I want to think about is this little angel."

Tyler drank some coffee and looked at her over the rim of the mug. "You know, I wouldn't have pegged you for a girl who falls in love so quickly."

Her gaze met his instantly. "I defy anyone not to love Cara the moment she smiles," she said and touched the baby's head gently. "Even someone as obviously jaded as you."

Tyler bit back a grin. "Jaded? I don't think anyone has ever called me that before."

"No?" Her brows rose. "You've just been called other things, right?" She paused for effect. "Cold, calculating, ruthless. My friend Kayla found out about you on the internet."

He smiled. "And was it interesting reading?"

"Some of it," she replied. "You're obviously successful at what you do."

"Yes," he said without modesty. "I am."

"Do you enjoy it?"

"Being a lawyer?" he queried and then shrugged. "I like winning. I'm not sure I'd call it enjoyment. I'd rather leave the enjoyment thing to other, more, shall we say, personal parts of my life."

She knew exactly what he meant and regarded him with a new kind of awareness. He wasn't sure how she could do that. It had been a long time since any woman had invaded his thoughts the way Brooke Laughton did. But there was something unavoidable about the effect she had on him.

"Are you flirting with me?" she asked bluntly.

Tyler grinned, thinking how he'd told himself he needed to stop doing that only minutes earlier. "I'm not exactly sure. If I was, would it be working?"

"Not one bit," she replied and focused her attention on the baby for a moment. When she looked up again her eyes were darker. "That would be a little foolish on my part, don't you think?"

"Probably," he said and drained his coffee mug and looked at the baby. "And mine. Considering the circumstances."

"Yes," she said quietly. "Cara is all that matters."

He nodded. "But, for the record, I'm not your enemy. I want what is best for Cara, just like you do."

"I know," she said and switched the baby onto her other knee. "That's all we really have in common."

His mouth twisted. "Well, except for the fact we're both single, straight and are going to be living together for the next week."

Put like that, it sounded impossibly intimate and Brooke's nerves were suddenly on high alert.

This is only about Cara...

And not Tyler Madden's sexy green eyes and broad shoulders. But Brooke quickly realized she was not immune to him. In fact, she was quite the opposite.

Stupid. Foolish. And absolutely out of the question.

But he *was* flirting with her. She was sure of it. Even if it made no sense at all. They were from different worlds. As opposite as two people could be. He was pure city boy and she was as country as a girl could get.

Brooke ignored the tight band of tension now squeezing at her temples and got to her feet. She passed Cara to him and took a few steps back. "I'll make her some dinner."

He nodded. "She'll go down in her crib with a bottle afterward."

Brooke managed a smile and spent the next twenty minutes busying herself with the food preparation and ignoring the man sitting at her dining table. He didn't seem to mind, though. He simply occupied himself by talking softly to the baby. His deep voice was oddly hypnotic and by the time she had Cara's meal prepared she was much more relaxed.

"Oh," she said as she came around the counter with Cara's dinner. "I've left a hat and a jacket for you hanging in the mudroom. They belonged to my ex. You're bigger than him, but the jacket should fit. That woolen coat of yours is a bit flashy for roughing it out on the range," she said and grinned übersweetly.

He nodded and turned Cara around as Brooke pulled a chair closer and sat down. She waited while he adjusted Cara's bib, watching the way he easily and naturally handled the baby. It uncurled something inside her and made her even more aware of him.

"She can hold the spoon and feed herself. Although we might need to consider protective clothing," he said as he looked up and smiled.

Brooke held the spoon in midair, conscious of how close she was to him. Their knees were almost touching and she pushed back the heat climbing through her limbs. "Huh?"

"Sometimes she likes to throw her food off the spoon."

Brooke's brows rose sharply and she looked at Cara's angelic expression. "I'm sure we'll be fine."

He chuckled lightly. "Don't say I didn't warn you."

Fifteen minutes later Brooke realized she should have heeded his cautioning. She had mashed pumpkin and peas splattered down the front of her clothes. As did Tyler. He also had it in his hair, over his arms and smeared across one cheek.

"So," she said and placed the bowl on the table. "I guess I should have listened."

He smiled, stood and held Cara against his chest. "I'll just get her cleaned up and put her down for the night— hopefully." He grinned, then stared down briefly at his T-shirt. "And then take a shower."

Brooke nodded and waited until he'd left the room before she took another breath. Being around Tyler was becoming increasingly difficult. There was so much energy between them.

Hah...it's not energy.

A silent, but outspoken voice taunted her.

It wasn't energy. It was heat. It was attraction. *Sex.*

Everything she'd avoided for the past two years.

She shook the idea off and cleaned up the kitchen, then hurried to her bedroom, ignoring the sound of Tyler's deep voice carrying up the hallway as he gently spoke to Cara, and shut herself inside her room. She quickly stripped off and headed for the small master bathroom, where she showered, dried herself as swiftly as she could and then changed into fresh jeans, tank top and then covered up with a long-sleeved chambray shirt that buttoned up to her throat.

When she left her room and made her way down the hall she heard the hiss of the shower in the main bathroom and quickly checked on Cara. The baby was already asleep, and looking at her made Brooke's heart roll over.

Please come home, Matt... Please come home so that Tyler doesn't take her away.

The idea of losing Cara made her ache inside. And with that thought she headed back to the kitchen, grabbed her cell phone and called her brother. It went to his voice mail and she left a message, this one more urgent than the last. Once she ended the call, Brooke sent a text for extra effect. This one telling Matt he *had* to come home. Now.

"Everything alright?"

She looked up. Tyler stood in the doorway, dressed in dark jeans and a pale gray sweater that highlighted every inch of his broad-shouldered torso, and Brooke swallowed back the sudden dryness in her throat. His hair was damp, his jaw clean shaven and he looked ridiculously handsome.

"Just calling my brother again," she said, figuring there was little point in denying it.

His brows narrowed fractionally. "Still no response?"

She shrugged. "Not yet. He probably hasn't checked his cell. I'll try again in the morning."

He stepped into the room, came around the counter and placed both hands on the countertop. "Brooke," Tyler said quietly. "Have you considered that perhaps your brother has received every one of your messages and is choosing to ignore them?"

She shook her head. "No. I know my brother. I'm sure he'll be in touch soon."

"I hope so. For Cara's sake. And yours."

Brooke's expression tightened. "You think I'm getting too attached to her. You want to take her away from me. Even though you know I would care for her, here… where she belongs."

He drew in a long breath. "You can't raise a child on good intentions. Cara needs—"

"Love," she said, cutting him off. "That's all a child really needs. Look," she said impatiently, "I understand that you think you need to stay all *business* about this whole thing. But this isn't some kind of corporate merger. This is about people. About *family*. It's about blood ties and DNA and…"

Brooke's words trailed off when she realized what she'd said. He looked at her oddly. Was he annoyed? Hurt? Angry? She couldn't tell…there was such impassive indifference in his expression. She didn't know him, couldn't gauge his moods.

"I'm sorry… I didn't mean that those things are *all* that matter in being a family," she said quickly, swallowing the discomfiture clawing at the throat. "I just… I just think…"

"Don't worry about it," he said and pushed himself off the counter.

"I've offended you?"

He stilled, crossed his arms and met her gaze. "No. As we've agreed, the only thing that's important is Cara's well-being. And your brother proving he is able to be the parent she deserves. That's if he shows up, of course. Which I'm seriously doubting he is going to do."

Panic etched across her skin. "You said you'd give him a week."

"I know what I said. And I will keep my word. But if Matt doesn't show, once the week is up I'll be taking Cara back to New York."

There was finality in his voice and it chilled her through to her bones. Brooke squared her shoulders and managed a tight smile. "I thought I'd make dinner. Any food allergies I should know about?"

"No. Except I don't like asparagus."

She grinned a little. "Me, either. Slimy little green sticks."

He pulled out a chair and sat down. "What else don't you like?"

"Champagne," she said and wrinkled her nose. "And because I can be a klutz, roller skates." She paused for effect. "But, I like imported beer and salted caramel popcorn and slow dancing."

"And horses?" he offered with a smile that was so sexy her knees weakened.

Brooke nodded. "They've been a big part of my life."

"You were very successful for a lot of years. Do you miss competing?"

"Yes," she admitted and sighed. "But I had to leave the competitive circuit when my parents died. It's a job that required a lot of traveling and I couldn't do both. This ranch has been in my family for five generations... I had to do what I could to keep it going."

His expression narrowed. "You said that you were having some troubles keeping the place afloat?"

Brooke's back straightened instantly. The last thing she wanted to do was get into her tale of woe about the ranch with Tyler. The less he knew, the better. "I said that?"

He shrugged one shoulder. "You inferred it."

Her suspicions rose. He was a lawyer. And a resourceful one, by all accounts. He had a file on her brother and no doubt she was a part of that. Of course he knew how things were. It was naive to think otherwise.

"I'm pretty sure you know exactly how things stand."

"I know some," he replied. "I know you've been fighting a rezoning issue."

"That's right. Up until a few months ago, Cedar River was actually two towns, separated by a river and a truckload of bureaucratic red tape. The town merged after a decade of negotiation."

"And?" he prompted.

"And that meant land rezoning for some people. I lost forty acres of my best grazing pasture."

"Is that all?"

She shrugged loosely. "I have a mortgage and creditors... and a long and complicated story you don't need to hear."

"Or you don't want to tell?"

"I'd like to keep my problems to myself...unless they affect my ability to adequately care for Cara," she said firmly, making sure he knew she wasn't about to back down in her determination to keep Cara at the ranch where she belonged, and long after he'd gone. "Which they don't."

One brow cocked up. "And the bank?"

"I'll keep them at bay," she replied coolly. "As I've done for the past few months."

His expression narrowed. "Could you actually lose the ranch?"

A familiar pain hit her squarely between the shoulders. Losing the ranch was the worst outcome imaginable. But it remained a very real possibility. She mustered every ounce of bravado she could. "I won't let that happen."

He watched her with such blistering intensity that Brooke could barely draw breath. There was an elemental strength about him, a kind of confidence she'd rarely encountered. Sure, when she'd been on the show circuit there had been plenty of cowboys who oozed charm and walked with a self-assured swagger...but Tyler Madden was different. There was nothing overt or obvious about him. He spoke quietly and didn't appear to waste words on pointless conversation. And he seemed kind and considerate, especially the way he interacted with Cara. It was an attractive quality and Brooke was becoming more and more drawn to him.

Which was foolhardy and completely out of the question, of course.

Right now, she had her ailing ranch, her orphaned niece and her AWOL brother to think about…and not a hot lawyer with a dimple to die for and broad shoulders that were way too tempting for her peace of mind. Especially since he held Cara's future in his hands.

"And my brother *will* come back," she said with more belief than she felt, but Brooke wasn't about to let him see otherwise. "I know Matt and I know he'll want to do what is right by his daughter once he knows about her."

Tyler shrugged in that loose way she was becoming accustomed to. "I hope he does. For everyone's sake. Cara needs a fully engaged parent, and not someone who'll bail when things get hard."

She gritted her teeth. "I need to have faith in him. Maybe you can live your life not believing in anything or anyone," she said stiffly. "But I can't."

One brow came up. "That's quite a judgment."

"I don't know you well enough to judge you, Tyler." Saying his name made her tremble inside. However, she continued speaking. "But I know my brother… I know that despite everything…despite the fact he hasn't been home for five years, I know he'll do what's right for Cara. He was a boy when he left, but now he's nearly twenty-four and a grown man…old enough to act with maturity and be a father to his daughter."

"Like I said, I hope he does."

Brooke turned back to her task and began whisking eggs to make triple cheese and green pepper omelets. Tyler offered to set the table and she nodded, sucking in a steadying breath when he came around the counter to collect silverware and the bread basket she'd filled with toasted slices of sourdough. And she tried to *not* think about how absurdly domestic the scene was. Other than her cousins Grady and Brant, he was the first man she'd had in her kitchen for over two years. He handled the task like he'd done it countless times before, and she figured he probably did everything with the same kind of confident ease and she envied that quality.

"Can you cook?" she asked as he set the table.

He looked up and grinned. "I can usually throw something edible together."

"I mean, do you cook at home?" she asked.

"On the weekends mostly," he replied. "I work long hours during the week."

Brooke dished out the omelets, picked up the plates and moved around the counter. "You live in the city?"

"Manhattan," he replied and took a plate and then waited for her to be seated before he sat down.

"An apartment?"

"Yes."

She gave a wry grin. "So, Cedar River and this ranch are literally a world away from what you know?"

"I lived in a small town in Nebraska until I was sixteen," he said and picked up a fork. "I know my way around a ranch house."

She'd bet her boots he'd know his way around anything.

"Can you ride a horse?"

"Yes."

"Are you one of those really annoying people who are good at everything?"

He met her gaze. "I guess time will tell."

Brooke regarded him thoughtfully. He had to have some flaws, some part of his character that was less than perfect. "Why haven't you gotten married?"

His mouth twisted. "That's kind of personal, don't you think?"

She shrugged lightly. "Just making conversation."

He didn't believe that any more than she did. "I guess I've never met anyone I've liked enough to want to spend the rest of my life with."

"You mean love?" she said.

"I mean *like*," he said quietly. "Love fades. It gets mixed up with attraction and desire and can make people act rashly."

Brooke held her fork midair. "That's a fairly grim view."

"Realistic," he replied, then twisted his mouth a little. "Did you love your ex-fiancé?"

"Of course."

"Did you *like* him?" he asked softy. "I mean, did you like him more than anyone else you've ever met? Was he the last person you wanted to see before you fell asleep at night? Or the first person you wanted to see when you woke up?"

Brooke stilled instantly. His words made her think. Had she *liked* Doyle? She wasn't sure. She certainly believed she'd loved him at the time and had nursed a broken heart long after he'd left. But looking back, she suspected there *was* something missing from their relationship. Otherwise, why would he have left so easily? There had been little resistance from him the moment his ex-girlfriend had come to town and announced they had a child together. Of course Brooke understood his desire to be a father to his son and had encouraged him to foster a relationship with his child…but she hadn't expected him to sprint out the door and discard her so easily.

"Are you okay?"

Brooke blinked, realizing there was moisture in her eyes and that Tyler Madden had witnessed them. She sucked in a deep breath. "I'm fine. And I suppose I must have liked him a little at the time, otherwise it might have made accepting his proposal a little awkward."

Tyler chuckled and the sound did something to her insides. He really was ridiculously sexy. And Brooke knew she had to stop thinking about him like that, or she was in danger of making a complete idiot of herself.

And she wasn't about to be a fool over a man ever again.

Chapter Five

Tyler stretched out on the bed and stared at the ceiling. It was early, not yet six thirty, but he'd been dozing off and on for over an hour. Cara had stirred a couple of times during the night and he'd gone to her each time he'd heard her whimpering through the static of the baby monitor. The mattress was lumpy and narrow—only a double bed. When he remembered the king-size comfort of the bed at O'Sullivans he wondered what kind of craziness had made him move into Brooke Laughton's ranch house.

Indigo eyes...

Yeah...he needed to forget all about her sultry eyes and sexy curves in a hurry.

Swinging out of bed, Tyler planted his feet on the floor. Cold air hit his bare arms and he grabbed the sweater from the end of the bed where he'd tossed it the night before, shoving his arms into the sleeves. Six days, he thought, and he was gone. If Matt Laughton didn't show he would be on his way home this time next week, back in his apartment, his office, his own bed and the life he'd put on hold because he'd made a promise to an old man and a dying girl.

He shook off the thought and finished getting dressed, pulling on jeans, socks and boots. Then he grabbed the baby monitor and left the room, checking on a sleeping Cara before he headed down the hall. The scent of freshly brewed coffee assailed his senses and he spotted an enameled pot sitting by the stove. A light was on, which meant Brooke was up, and he ducked back out into the hall and checked the front living room. The room was empty so he returned to the kitchen, placed the monitor on the counter, poured himself a mug of coffee and stood by the window, looking out over the yard. Snow was falling, a little heavier than the day before, and when he noticed that his rental car was covered in a thick layer of the stuff he made a mental note to get outside as soon as Cara was awake and fed and clear the snow off.

A flash of color near the stables caught his attention. It was Brooke. In jeans, pink rubber boots and a bright pink hooded anorak she looked like a lovely beacon set against the backdrop of snow and stables. It made him smile, although he had no idea why. Maybe because she didn't seem to be the kind of woman who would favor the color pink. She carried a small basket and a pitchfork and the dogs were jumping around her excitedly.

He stayed where he was, absorbed by the image of her determined strides and straight back. There was something about the way she held herself that captivated him. The tilt of her chin, the square of her shoulders, the slight swing of her arms…it evoked a picture of a resilient, independent woman and someone very much in her element outdoors. There was nothing pretentious about Brooke…nothing fake…nothing other than strength and integrity in her demeanor. She was a good person. And realizing that fact made an already complicated situation even more so.

The night before he'd gotten to know her a little better over a rubbery omelet, witnessing her mood shift from tense to humorous and companionable and then to a little sad. There had been tears in her eyes when she'd spoken about her ex-fiancé and he didn't like the way those tears had made him feel. Helpless, for one, especially when she'd quickly finished the meal and then soon after disappeared to her room pleading a headache and the need for rest. He'd helped her clean up and then headed to his own room feeling like they'd somehow ended the evening on a sour note. He wasn't sure why it should matter, but the idea still kept him tossing and turning for most of the night, in between getting up to check on Cara.

Tyler didn't want to be at odds with Brooke. She was his way of connecting with Matt and seeing if the younger man could actually be a parent to Cara. They needed to get along. Which meant he had to make more of an effort to be civil and not so prickly. But she set him on edge with her deep purple eyes and obvious disapproval.

When she came back through the mudroom about ten minutes later, Tyler was on his second cup of coffee and ignored the way his blood warmed when she trudged into the kitchen, boots off, tugging at the chin cord on her anorak. Her cheeks were pink and her lovely hair was escaping its ponytail. He looked at her feet and smiled to himself at the sight of her fuchsia-colored socks.

"I thought you like to sleep in on Sunday mornings?" he asked as he moved around the countertop, then grabbed a mug from the cupboard and poured her coffee, adding milk and sugar.

She shrugged out of her coat and hung it on a hook by the door. "I do," she said and pointed to the clock on the wall. "I was up at six…that's an hour later than usual and quite decadent for me."

He frowned. "You start your day at five a.m.? Are you nuts?"

She laughed loudly and it made him grin. "I have six horses, two dogs, a few dozen head of cattle and seven chickens…so lazy mornings are not on my radar. But don't hold back here, Tyler…say it how you see it."

"As a rule, I generally do."

She pushed back some of her wayward hair and took the mug. Their knuckles touched and he was startled by the instant response he felt across his skin. He tried to recall the last time he'd had such an intense reaction to a woman. Maybe never. It didn't make sense. She wasn't his type. He liked brunettes, not blondes. He liked professional women who were immaculately groomed and wore high-fashion stiletto heels. Not freckle-faced cowgirls with flushed cheeks and who wore silly pink socks.

She was looking up at him, her expression curious, and her chin, defiant and determined, rose in that way he was becoming used to. Tyler swallowed hard, felt tension and awareness snake up his spine as he tried to tamp down what he was feeling for her. But to no avail. It was there, in the space between them and in the molecules of air they shared. And he knew she felt it, too. He also knew she was trying just as hard to ignore it. After all, being attracted to each other was futile. He was leaving in less than a week and she had a whole lot going on in her life and couldn't afford the distraction. It should have been enough to make both of them step away. But they didn't.

His gaze moved to her mouth and he noticed how her lips parted fractionally, as though she knew exactly what he was thinking about. Which was kissing her. Long and hard and hot.

Desire coursed through his blood, quickly scrambling his brain. He moved suddenly and backed into the table, feeling simultaneously turned on and foolish.

I need to get control of this...and fast.

"Heard from your brother yet?" he asked coolly, shifting the subject and watching her expression change from curious to annoyed.

She stepped back and shrugged lightly. "He hasn't answered my texts yet."

"He's got six more days."

"So you keep reminding me," she said, her eyes flashing as she sipped her coffee.

He pressed on. "For Cara's sake I have to put a time frame around this, Brooke. If your brother returns your calls, then perhaps we can resolve this situation quickly. Which would be better for everyone."

"Everyone?" she echoed. "Are you missing the city already?"

"I have a life to get back to," he replied, ignoring the irritation crawling up his back. She certainly had a way of getting under his skin. "As do you. And frankly, I don't want the reason I'm here to get mixed up with anything else."

She glared at him. "Mixed up? What does that mean?"

Tyler wasn't sure how he could respond without sounding like a self-centered fool. But he was pretty sure she knew exactly what he meant. "I think you know."

He watched, fascinated as color crept up her neck and smacked her cheeks. Her eyes glittered vibrantly. "That's...absurd."

"Is it?"

She sucked in a sharp breath. "If you're insinuating that I'm...that I think you're...that I'm interested in *anything* other than my niece, then you are way off the mark."

He didn't believe her. She didn't look like she believed it, either. Tyler had his fair share of ego, but he'd never considered himself particularly egotistical. And if Brooke was too uncomfortable to acknowledge what was building between them, then he wasn't going to push the subject. "Okay, fair enough. Just making sure we're on the same page in regard to this situation."

"Is that lawyer code for making me feel like crap?"

Tyler stilled. "That's not the first time you've aimed a hit at my profession. Do you have a thing against lawyers?"

Her chin came up. "I have a thing against being made to feel as though I'm on trial," she said heatedly. "As though I have to impress you. Yesterday you said we were on the same side… This morning you're behaving like a complete jerk."

The truth in her words burned through him. She was right. It was Matt Laughton who needed to prove he could be a parent to Cara… It was unfair to expect the same of Brooke. But she got under his skin in ways he hadn't been prepared for. Obviously the less time they spent together, the better.

"Unintentional," he said and drained his coffee mug when he heard the baby through the monitor. "I need to check on Cara."

She nodded. "I'll get her bottle ready. And perhaps some oatmeal?"

Tyler nodded. "Sure. Like I said, she'll eat most things. Be back soon."

He left the room, eager to get away from her. And feeling for one of the few times in his life like he was in way over his head.

* * *

By the time Tyler returned to the kitchen with Cara in his arms, Brooke had had a ten-minute reprieve to pull herself together plus the opportunity to dilute the irritation coursing through her blood. Damn him. It was as though every conversation they had turned into a sparring match. Brooke knew she needed to keep a lid on her emotions and not allow him to see how he affected her. The night before he'd seen her tears…this morning her temper. When what she really needed to do was keep calm and try to get along with him for the sake of her niece. Tyler held all the cards. He could leave at any moment and she would lose the opportunity to get to know Cara…which was unthinkable.

With that thought Brooke texted her brother again.

"Everything okay?" he asked and settled Cara in the high chair he'd set up the afternoon before.

"Just fine," she said and slipped her cell phone into her pocket. "Oatmeal is ready, bottle almost done."

He nodded and settled back in a chair while Brooke finished getting the bottle ready and then supervised Cara's breakfast. The baby splattered food on the floor, the high chair and down her bib. And despite the palpable tension between Tyler and herself, Brooke was captivated by Cara's laughter and enjoyment as the baby smeared oatmeal everywhere she could reach.

When she was done, Tyler suggested she take Cara into the front living room while he cleaned up. She didn't bother resisting the idea. Brooke wanted to spend as much time as possible with her niece and he deserved to do house chores after behaving like a conceited horse's ass earlier. What was he thinking? That Brooke was so enamored with his green eyes and broad shoulders she'd forget why he was at her home in the first place? So, maybe she had spared him the odd appreciative look. She was a red-blooded woman, after all. But that's all it was…a few curious looks and an awareness of his obvious physical appeal. He was sexy as sin. But that's where her interest ended. If they'd met at a bar or a party and connected in some way, she may have been tempted to come out of sexual hibernation and pursue whatever road the attraction took. But they hadn't met that way. And there was too much at stake for Brooke to get distracted by physical attraction for a man she hardly knew. A man who represented everything she feared most.

It was better to ignore it. Better to forget it.

Besides, he obviously had no real interest in her. Whatever he was thinking, Brooke had no illusions about herself. She was average in the beauty stakes and had been out of the loop for so long when it came to men she had no real idea how to act around one. Plus, she was essentially a tomboy. Handy with a pair of fence cutters or a hammer and nails, but spent little time preening or marketing herself as an available woman. Doyle had always said he liked her low-maintenance, down-to-earth ways. As had the one other boyfriend she'd had before him. But a man like Tyler—a big-city lawyer with the reputation of a wolf—wouldn't be content with a country-bred woman…he'd prefer Park Avenue style. Not that she cared one bit. He could prefer whoever he wanted.

"Brooke?"

She turned once she'd settled Cara on the couch with a bottle. Tyler stood in the doorway, one shoulder resting against the jamb. There was something so elementally masculine about him and she remembered how only days ago she'd thought him some kind of pretty boy with little substance. But he wasn't. There was an air of quiet confidence around him that affected her in a way she couldn't quite define. Finding him attractive was one thing...*liking* him, another thing altogether. She didn't have the time to like anyone.

Brooke took a deep breath. "Cara seems settled," she said and gestured to the baby lying restfully on the sofa, her bottle between her tiny hands.

"She is," he said and nodded. "You're good with her. I've not seen her take to anyone as easily as she has taken to you."

"Like who?" Brooke asked curiously.

"Her last nanny in particular."

Brooke bit back a smile. "You mean *you* didn't take to the nanny, right?"

He pushed himself off the door frame and stepped into the room. "She was like a drill instructor. And glacial. Poor kid didn't get an ounce of affection from the woman."

Brooke's heart contracted. "I defy anyone not to love this little girl. She's so adorable and sweet. She chatters a lot, but does she say any actual words?"

He shook his head. "Not really. If Yelena was alive I'm sure she'd be saying *mama* and probably trying to verbalize more than she does. Lately she's become a little withdrawn. Natural, I suppose, considering what she's lost. And the upheaval of coming all this way. She traveled well, but still, it's a long haul for a baby."

"I think she's remarkable," Brooke said and dropped into the sofa beside her. "And I'm so glad she's here, so I can get to know her."

"It's just a shame she comes as a package deal, right?"

Brooke met his gaze. "You're not all bad, I'm sure."

"I have my uses I suppose."

Warmth crawled over her skin, despite the fact it was a cool morning. "No doubt. You said you could cook."

"Better than you, at least."

She was immediately affronted, but remained good-humored. "I'm a good cook."

He shook his head and grinned. "Ah...no, you're not."

His candor amused her and she smiled a little. "I've never had anyone complain before."

"Perhaps they know you have a shotgun by the front door."

Brooke laughed and was amazed at how good it felt. There had been too few laughs in her life over the past couple of years. When she'd first met Doyle she'd been drawn to his energy and ability to make her laugh. Make her cry, as it turned out in the end. Losing her parents, Doyle and in a way her brother, had hardened her inside and made her wary of being vulnerable to anyone.

But she felt vulnerable in that moment... To Cara. And to the man who, through circumstance, was now living in her home.

"I'm a lousy shot anyhow," she said and shrugged. "Probably on par with my cooking."

He smiled. "I wasn't being critical."

"Sure seemed like it. But don't worry... I'm not the kind of girl to take offense, Tyler."

He moved farther into the room and stood by the fireplace. "No? What kind of girl are you?"

"Tough as nails," she replied quickly and felt heat rise up over her skin again. "Thick-skinned. Robust. Resilient."

"That's quite a list," he said and met her gaze evenly. "Although, your skin is actually quite lovely."

Brooke's cheeks burned foolishly. "I have freckles."

"Yes," he said quietly. "I know."

Brooke felt the glow of his words spread from the roots of her hair through to the soles of her feet. A quiet, taunting voice warned her that she was way out of her league…that she had no idea how to handle a man like Tyler Madden. She knew she had to put an end to whatever was going on between them. "Stop flirting with me."

He laughed and the sound reached her way down. "I'm not," he said easily as he walked to the window and looked outside. "Not really. You're just—"

"The only woman within a ten-mile radius," she offered, cutting him off. "I get it."

He turned around and his green eyes glittered brilliantly. "You do?"

She shrugged with as much indifference as she could muster, considering his gaze was piercing through her. "Sure… Cedar River isn't exactly Grand Central Station in the opposite-sex department."

He laughed, as though he found her hilarious, when Brooke was entirely serious. She scowled and that only seemed to amplify his amusement. Brooke was about to lock horns with him but glanced toward the baby first, relieved to see Cara looking content and a little sleepy. She might only be a year old, but Brooke certainly didn't want the baby picking up on any tension between herself and Tyler.

"Is something funny?" she asked tightly, reining in her irritation.

"I didn't come to Cedar River looking to get laid, hooked up, married or otherwise," he replied drily. "And if you're inferring that I find you attractive because you're the only woman in the immediate vicinity, you're wrong."

She blinked. "You think I'm attractive?"

He shrugged. "Of course. But it doesn't really matter, does it?" he pointed out. "I'm here for one reason," he said and gestured toward the baby. "With no intention of complicating things by acting on *anything*. We're both smart people, Brooke…too smart to muddy the waters."

She wanted to feel indignation, outrage and plain old disbelief that he could stand before her and say the words so calmly, without so much as a blip in his deep timbre, his voice smooth. But her outrage was diluted by the realization that the sexual awareness she'd been experiencing for the past couple of days was mutual. Of course he was right…nothing could happen. Nothing *would* happen. But she couldn't help thinking that in other circumstances, things might be very different.

Brooke watched him, saw him plant his hands on his hips, and watched how his shoulders rose up and down as he breathed. His arms were well-defined and muscular and she couldn't help thinking how much she'd like to feel them wrapped around her…even for a moment. There was strength in Tyler, the kind she hadn't been around for a long time. Plus kindness and integrity. Only a man who possessed both those qualities would have traveled from the other side of the country to try and connect Cara with her father.

"You're right," she said quietly, and then decided to dig a little deeper. "Tell me about Cara's great-grandfather."

He frowned. "Ralph?"

She nodded. "I'd like to know how you met."

"I told you," he said flatly. "He was my court-appointed lawyer. We became friends and once I decided on a career in law he became my mentor."

"He must be very proud of you," she remarked. "Considering all you have achieved."

"I couldn't say."

He looked tense and Brooke was amazed how easily she could read his expression. "I don't mean by the money or the fancy apartment. I mean by how you are with Cara. Bringing her here, caring for her the way you do…he must trust and respect you to leave her in your care. You're remarkable with her and she lights up whenever she sees you… I imagine it will be hard for you to let her go."

He glanced toward the baby, who was happily lying on the sofa, chugging on the bottle. "I want what is best for her, that's all. If that turns out to be your brother, then I will have no trouble leaving her in his care. Cara deserves to have a family and a parent who puts her above all others. If Matt can do that, if he can prove he is prepared to be a real father to her, then I'll relinquish my guardianship. But frankly, the fact he hasn't even responded to your calls demonstrates a serious lack of reliability."

Brooke's insides tightened and she asked the question that was burning in her heart. "Would you consider leaving her here with me?"

No.

Tyler held his tongue. He didn't want to get into another argument with Brooke about her suitability as a caregiver for her niece. She had the best intentions, he was sure…but it took more than that to raise a child.

"We'll see what happens."

"I am capable of caring for a child," she murmured and touched Cara's head.

"I don't doubt it," he replied. "I'm sure you'll make a fine mother one day."

She met his gaze head-on. There was a flash of hurt in her eyes that made his insides contract. He'd hit a nerve with his comment, he was sure of it. He didn't know why, but he could speculate. She was thirty-two and childless… maybe her clock was ticking.

"Have I said something I shouldn't?" he asked quietly, feeling about as sensitive as a rock.

She shook her head and shrugged a little. "No, of course not. So," she said, changing the subject, "I have some fencing to get to today and should be gone for a few hours. Make yourself at home while I'm gone. The TV remote is on the coffee table and the refrigerator is full."

"Fencing?" he queried and glanced toward the window. "In this weather? It's still snowing out there."

She shrugged again, firmer this time. "The work on a ranch doesn't stop because of a little snow, city boy."

"Is that another crack at my profession?" he asked and raised his brows. "I imagine they have lawyers in small towns, including this one."

"Oh, there is," she said and grinned sweetly. "But he's no Harvard Law man like yourself. And he's about as effective as a wet sock."

"I went to Columbia," he corrected. "And if your lawyer's a dud, get someone else."

"Werner is all I can afford. And he's nice enough, but he's just easily spooked."

"Spooked?" he queried.

She shook her head. "Nothing... I shouldn't have said that."

"It's a little late to be coy, don't you think? And if you're in some kind of legal trouble, perhaps I can help."

She looked as though it was the last thing she wanted. "I'm not in trouble," she assured him and patted Cara's chest gently. "It's under control and my lawyer is trying to keep the wolves at bay the best he can."

"The wolves?" he echoed. "You mean the bank?"

She half nodded and got to her feet. "And any interested parties who think I'm vulnerable at the moment."

He didn't imagine Brooke Laughton scared easily. But

he wanted to know, regardless of his usual caution of knowing too much or getting too close to someone outside the boundaries of his work. Because, despite the situation with Cara, talking with Brooke didn't feel like it was part of a job or a case. "Tell me what's going on."

"No."

"I'm not your enemy," he said softly. "And I'm a very good lawyer."

Her indigo eyes flashed. "And modest."

"In my experience professional modesty is counterproductive. My clients need to know I can confidently represent them at all times…even when it seems hopeless."

Her chin jolted up. "Clients who can afford you, of course."

"I've done my share of pro bono work, Brooke. And you can be assured that anything you say will remain confidential."

"I can't. It's complicated," she insisted. "And no one's business."

She got to her feet and walked around the sofa, arms crossed, back straight. Tyler watched her intently, absorbed by the graceful way she moved, like she was in no particular hurry. Maybe that's what attracted him… the way she seemed calm and rock solid. Sure, she had a temper, but she mostly kept it under wraps and he admired that about her.

When she got to the main window she stared out for a few seconds before turning back to him. Her eyes were bright, and there was pure frustration in her expression… like she wasn't sure what she wanted to say. Admitting he was attracted to her probably hadn't been the smartest move, but he didn't want it to be an elephant in the room whenever they were together. Again, he marshaled his determination to ignore his emotions and focus only on business—no matter how difficult a task that might prove to be.

"Brooke," he said softly. "If your brother doesn't show up I have to make a decision about Cara's future. I'd like to make that decision knowing all the facts."

Her chin tilted. "I'm not on trial here, Counselor."

"No," he replied. "You've made it clear that you think Matthew will show up and be a father to Cara. But it's my decision, Brooke, and not a given. So the more I know, the better your chances."

She sucked in a deep breath and glared at him. She was clearly unhappy, and looked as though she was backed into a corner. Tyler felt a twinge of guilt hit him between the shoulder blades. But he was right to demand answers when Cara's future was at stake.

He watched as Brooke pushed back her shoulders and headed for the door. But she stopped in the doorway, her back straight and tense. After a moment she spoke.

"Okay," she said, not turning. "I'll tell you everything. But later."

Then she left the room and Tyler didn't move until he heard the front door close.

Chapter Six

Brooke had always believed that hard work was an antidote for stress and tension. And she needed stress relief after her last conversation with Tyler.

So, he thinks I'm attractive and he's blackmailed me into telling him all my business.

Pulling her shirt collar up, she trudged toward the stables. She'd been too wound up when she left the house to remember her coat and was grateful she had another hanging on a hook near the stable door. Grabbing it off the peg, she slipped into it and closed the buttons.

I don't have time for this kind of drama.

She was too sensible. Too levelheaded. Too busy trying to keep everything afloat, including herself. After her parents' deaths she'd stopped competing professionally on the rodeo circuit and returned home, with Doyle, and was filled with determination to continue working the ranch as her father had done. For a few months everything had seemed like it would work out—she made plans with Doyle to continue her father's legacy. But her plans quickly unraveled. Without Sky Dancer there was no breeding program and no income. Bills began piling up and creditors started calling night and day. Eighteen months later Doyle was gone, too. Since then she'd been treading water. Hoping. Praying. Waiting for it to all come crashing down while she tried to work out a way to salvage the only home she'd ever known. The only lifeline she had was to sell...but that was unthinkable. The ranch was in her blood and her bones and she wouldn't let it go without giving the fight of her life.

It was bitterly cold outside and for a few self-indulgent seconds she thought about being inside, curled up on the sofa in front of the fire, perhaps reading a book or having a quiet, relaxed conversation with someone.

With Tyler.

She shook the crazy idea from her thoughts. Finding each other attractive was one thing, acting on it was another thing altogether. Of course, she'd said she would tell him everything about the ranch and the accident... and she would. But for the next few hours she had to work out a way to get her attraction for Tyler out of her system.

Easy.

No problem.

Consider it done!

By the time she finished loading her truck with fencing gear she was sure she'd gotten over whatever it was that made her waste time thinking about Tyler's green eyes and broad shoulders. And then she had another three hours to chastise herself while she drove the fence line and repaired several posts. Brooke liked the work and never felt out of her depth when she was outdoors. Inside activities were always more of a chore. Recently she'd been a bridesmaid at her cousin Grady's wedding, and had felt so out of her comfort zone she was sure she'd had sweaty palms the entire day. Dressing up and wearing makeup and fancy clothes had never been her thing. Horses, wide-open spaces, jeans and a pair of comfy boots were more her style. Which was why thinking about Tyler Madden as anything other than Cara's guardian was plain old crazy.

By the time she got back to the stables it was half past ten and the snow had stopped falling. She packed the gear away and haltered her old palomino mare, Sharnah. The horse was twenty-nine, but still in excellent health and Brooke took her out for a gentle ride once a week or so. She tacked the mare up, got into the saddle and headed out for a half-hour amble across the meadow.

When she returned she felt better. More relaxed, more like herself. Until she spotted Tyler waiting by the corral, dressed in jeans, a blue checked shirt, boots, Stetson and the sheepskin coat she'd left out for him. He certainly filled out the clothes better than her ex-fiancé ever had. If the image wasn't sexy enough, the fact he held Cara in his arms completed the picture and made her heart pound. The baby wore a hooded pink anorak with matching leggings and tiny mittens and looked so adorable Brooke was suddenly breathless.

"Hi," she said as she eased Sharnah to a halt beside the corral.

"Hi yourself," he said and propped a gurgling Cara on one hip. "Enjoy your ride?"

Brooke nodded and then dismounted. "Yes…there's something special about riding in the snow."

He smiled. "This old girl looks as though she's seen a fair bit of snow in her days."

"This is Sharnah," she explained and rubbed the mare gently on the muzzle. "And we've been together since I was seven years old."

"That's quite a history," he said and moved closer to the horse so that Cara could touch the mare's neck with exploring fingers. "I take it she's something of a favorite around here?"

Brooke loosened the girth. "You could say that. She's Sky Dancer's mother. My dad bought her when she was four years old with a colt at foot."

He patted the mare's neck and her gaze was instantly drawn to his hand smoothing down the horse's coat. He had nice hands, she thought. Large and strong, not callused and rough like Doyle's had been.

"Do you ride her often?" he asked.

"No. Just enough to keep her fit. She still enjoys getting out and when the day comes that I think she's not enjoying it, I'll happily see her permanently retired. I have several good mounts if you're interested in having a ride while you're here."

"I think I'll keep my feet on the ground," he said and grinned as he stepped closer. "Unless you have work you need done."

"No," she said and eased the bit and bridle off Sharnah's head. "I have things under control."

He sucked in a sharp breath and went to speak, but Cara suddenly silenced them both. She reached forward and grasped Brooke's hand, wrapping tiny fingers around hers as she mumbled a few words that made no sense, and yet, spoke volumes. Brooke's heart flipped over instantly. It was such a simple thing, but the love she felt toward her niece in that moment was incredible. She looked up and saw that Tyler was watching her intently. He saw the connection, she was sure of it.

In that moment she had everything she wanted... everything she'd dreamed of. Of course, it wasn't real. Tyler was virtually a stranger and Cara wasn't her child…but if she closed her eyes, if she let her imagination get the better of her, it actually felt more real than anything ever had.

Emotion swelled her throat and she swallowed hard. "Please…" she whispered, saying what was in her heart. "Don't take her away."

For a moment Brooke wasn't sure he heard her. His expression was unreadable. Unfathomable. But then he raised his palm and cupped her cheek, so gently it was as though he'd done it countless times before. Brooke couldn't breathe. Couldn't move. There was electricity in his touch. And tenderness and compassion, too. Because he knew, she was sure, how important Cara had become to her. With the baby between them there was a kind of primal connection circling around them. In that instant it was as though they were the only three people on the planet. The snow, the silence, the solitude… all of it seemed to wrap them in a bubble for the briefest of moments.

His touch should have sent her running for the hills. Or leaping back. But it didn't. Whatever was burgeoning between them, with that one simple gesture it jumped ten paces forward. She wanted to press closer, be closer, stay closer. She wanted to feel his arms around her. And more. There was something so magnetic in his gaze that she couldn't have broken free no matter how much the practical part of her brain was telling her to.

"I can't promise you that," he said quietly, gently rubbing his thumb along her jaw. "I wish I could."

With those words the moment disappeared as quickly as it had come. Brooke sucked in a deep breath and stepped sideways. Cara cooed and laughed and Brooke's attention quickly focused on the baby. But the tension remained, swirling around them, making her loathe him and like him at the same time. She was about to pull on every ounce of her good sense and tell him to go to the devil when she spotted a car coming down the driveway.

"Expecting company?" Tyler asked when he saw her expression as she noticed the vehicle.

Brooke shook her head, slipping a halter onto Sharnah and tying her to the post. "No," she said. But she knew the truck. And the occupant. "I'll be right back."

She strode across the yard, knees incxplicably shaking. The logo on the side of the truck made her experience a familiar dread. The P & P Ranch. One of the largest in the county. Ruled over by Frank Pritchard and his no-good stepson, Devlin. But it wasn't Frank or Devlin who got out of the car. It was Will Serrato—foreman of the P & P. When the vehicle came to a halt he uncurled his six-foot-something frame out of the truck. The dogs raced up and jumped around, sensing no threat. Despite the fact he worked for Pritchard, Will wasn't a bad sort of man. But he still belonged to the enemy camp.

"'Mornin,' Brooke," he said and tilted his hat.

"Hi," she said cautiously. "What do you want, Will?"

"Boss would like to talk to you."

"Then why isn't he here?" she asked.

His handsome face creased into a wry smile. "Might have somethin' to do with the shotgun you had at your side the last time he stopped by."

"I never threatened anyone," she reminded him. "Despite the fact he was trespassing on private property."

Will didn't flinch. "So, about the meeting?"

"I'm not interested."

He named a monetary sum, way less than she knew was fair. "That's his offer, Brooke."

"The Laughton Ranch isn't for sale," she said flatly. "Any part of it. And certainly not to Frank Pritchard.

Or to anyone connected with him. You've wasted a trip, Will."

"Better to sell now than when the bank forecloses, don't you think?" he said and raised a brow. "You'll get a better price."

Annoyance snaked up her spine. "You should leave. And tell your boss not to make any more offers because I'm not interested."

Will shrugged a broad shoulder and tilted his hat again. "I'll pass on your message."

"Everything okay here, Brooke?"

Tyler's voice jerked her gaze sideways. She hadn't heard him approach, but was torn between being foolishly pleased to have him by her side, and despairing that he might work out how deep in trouble she really was. Not that she felt threatened by Will Serrato in any way, as the good-looking cowboy had always been polite and respectful toward her.

"Everything is fine," she assured the man now standing at her side. She noticed the pulse in his cheek was beating rapidly and Cara was snuggled close to his chest. If she'd ever had the idea a baby in his arms could be emasculating, she was wrong. He'd never looked stronger or more ready to come to her defense. "He was just leaving."

She didn't introduce them and instead called the dogs to her side and turned to walk away. She heard the vehicle door slam shut and within seconds the truck was heading back down the driveway, leaving snow and mud churning in its wake.

Tyler caught up with her quickly and asked the obvious question. "Who was that?"

Back at the corral, Brooke unclipped Sharnah's girth strap. "No one."

"Old boyfriend?"

She glanced sideways and scowled. "Hardly. If you must know he is the minion of my mortal enemy."

His mouth twisted. "You have a mortal enemy?"

She pulled the saddle off. "I was being dramatic."

He shifted Cara onto his other hip and touched her shoulders. "Well, how about you be less dramatic and more honest."

Brooke turned to face him, so close that the edge of his jacket brushed hers. "His name is Will Serrato."

"And?" Tyler prompted.

"He's the foreman of the P & P Ranch," she explained. "Which is one of the two biggest spreads in this county."

"And?" he asked again.

"And his boss wants to buy part of my ranch," she said hotly.

"Is it for sale?"

"No," she replied. "And it never will be. So I sent him on his way. End of story."

He dropped his hand and stared at her…through her… into her…his green eyes seeing all her fears, all her regret…all her pain. She was sure of it. He was a lawyer, and by all accounts one of the best around. He questioned people for a living. Of course he would be able to see through her paltry attempts to stay strong and in control.

"I'm not buying it, Brooke," he said bluntly. "There's more to this than you're letting on. And I'm pretty sure it's got something to do with the bank threatening to foreclose, the accident that killed your parents *and* your missing-in-action brother."

He was right. It was all tangled up together and was one unholy mess.

"I said I would tell you," she replied as she unclipped Sharnah's lead. "And I will. Just not now."

His expression narrowed. "If you want a shot at keeping Cara," he said and touched the baby's head gently, "then I want the truth. All of it. Not some abridged version. Everything. You decide, Brooke."

Then he turned and walked off toward the house.

Tyler wasn't sure what was making him madder—Brooke's reluctance to talk, or his own interest in knowing her problems. Sure, part of his job required inquisition and having questions answered. But this was different. This *felt* different. This felt like involvement. Something he *never* did. Of course, he didn't like the idea that he'd pretty much blackmailed her into telling him. But he needed to know. He *wanted* to know. And if being ruthless got him what he wanted, so be it.

He gave Cara a drink and put her down for a nap. And then he waited in the living room for Brooke to return. It was a nice room, tastefully decorated. He glanced around the room. There was still no tree. Funny, but he would have pegged Brooke as someone who liked Christmas and all the festive nonsense that went with it. He never bothered with it himself and most years spent the day alone, usually declining any of the invitations he received from friends or colleagues to join their families. Tyler was used to his own company over the holidays. Occasionally he would go to Nebraska to spend Christmas with his parents, but he hadn't done that for several years.

Half an hour later he heard the door to the mudroom creak, and then her booted heels clicking over the polished timber floors as she headed down the hallway and into the living room. She stood behind the sofa and sucked in a couple of deep breaths.

"Okay," she said, hands on hips, indigo eyes ablaze. "I'm here. Ask away."

Tyler shifted his position on the love seat by the window and rested his elbows on his knees. "How much financial trouble are you in?"

"I have two months to find the mortgage back payments. After that the bank will foreclose."

He nodded. "And will you be able to find the funds?"

She shrugged lightly. "I plan to sell off most of my cattle. My cousin Grady is happy to take them off my hands for a good price."

"Will that be enough?" he queried.

"It will help…maybe give me time for an extension."

He nodded again. "And your mortal enemy…what does he have to do with it?"

She sighed. "I told you how up until recently Cedar River used to be two separate towns, right?" she asked, but didn't wait for his reply. "And like most small towns there are prominent families…some through wealth, some through reputation. Like the O'Sullivans, who own the big hotel in town and commercial property on both sides of the river. And then there are the Pritchards, Frank and his stepson, who own cattle and half the grazing land in the county."

"And where do you come in?"

"When the towns merged there was some land rezoning. I lost forty acres of my best grazing land that went to the Pritchard ranch, which sits south of this place. To the east is the big Culhane spread…it's a horse ranch mostly. Then there's me, kind of stuck in the middle." She sighed heavily. "But I have a strip of the best grazing land in the county that wasn't part of the rezoning… and that's the piece of dirt that Pritchard wants. It runs along the river and since the Pritchard ranch doesn't have the underground water table that the Culhanes and I do, he wants to get his hands on it."

Tyler sat back. So far, everything made sense. "So, what's his offer?"

She told him the figure as she came around the sofa and sat down. "It wouldn't matter what he offered. I won't sell."

"I don't know much about land value, but that seems like a low offer."

"It is," she said. "But the Pritchards aren't known for their generosity. Only their self-righteous belief that they can do whatever they want, whenever they want. But I won't be bullied."

"Of course not," Tyler said in agreement. "However, if the offer was fair and equitable would you consider it?"

"No," she said quickly.

Tyler frowned. "Why not?"

She looked toward the ground before meeting his gaze. "It's complicated."

He leaned forward. "We agreed you wouldn't give me the abridged version, remember?"

"Okay," she said, twisting her hands in her lap and clearly frustrated. "It goes back to the accident that killed my folks. Do you remember how I told you the other day that there was another car involved?"

"Of course."

"That car was…" She trailed off, stalling for a moment. "That car was driven by Frank Pritchard's daughter. She's some kind of musical prodigy and lives in Italy, I believe. She comes home once or twice a year to see her father and stepbrother. It was her car Matt saw on the road that day. Her car that was on the *wrong* side of the road."

Tyler leaned forward a little more. "Why wasn't any of this in the police report?"

She shrugged. "Because she was a *Pritchard.* And no one would believe my brother. When I confronted the old man about it he said I could never prove it...and he was right. It would have been Matt's word against hers. A genius from one of the richest families in the county against a teenage boy who'd already had his fair share of trouble with the law. In the end, Matt was charged with vehicular manslaughter, got a fine and a suspended sentence, and lost his license for five years. And Raina Pritchard headed back to Italy and to her symphony. But *I* know Frank Pritchard knows the truth," she said passionately and hooked a thumb toward her chest. "I feel it in here. I also know there is nothing I can do about it. And his insulting offer for my land is his arrogant way of letting me know he can do whatever he wants, without consequence."

Tyler watched her, saw her flashing eyes and pink cheeks and trembling chin and figured she was just a few more words away from either crying or throwing something. It made him uneasy. He didn't want to see her cry. He didn't want to see her unhappy. But he pressed on, trying to get to all of the truth.

"Are you refusing to sell because of pride?" he asked quietly. "Even though it would keep the bank at bay?"

Her jaw tightened instantly. "Even then," she said hotly. "It's the principle of the thing."

He couldn't help smiling a little. "Principles won't get your ranch solvent again, though, will it?"

"You think I should sell?"

"I think," he said with emphasis, "that you should do what is best for you and the ranch you want to keep. If that's selling to Pritchard, or to someone else, then it's worth considering."

She got to her feet and paced the room. "Ignoring the fact that the idea of selling to him makes my teeth hurt, he will never increase his offer because in some twisted way he thinks he has me on the ropes."

"Then let him know that he doesn't," Tyler suggested. "Make a counteroffer."

"I've been down that road. My lawyer says that—"

"It sounds like your lawyer is either lazy or incompetent. Or both."

She stilled instantly as he cut her off. "You know, I don't think I've ever known anyone who gives their opinion so freely or as regularly as you." Her eyes flashed brilliantly and she offered an overly sweet smile. "No wonder you're such a success in the courtroom…where I'll bet you enjoy hearing the sound of your own voice over and over."

He laughed loudly, trying to remember the last time someone had called him out as an overbearing know-it-all. Maybe never. But Brooke Laughton didn't mind telling him what she thought of him. And he wasn't insulted. On the contrary, he found her candidness fascinating.

"You know, there's something incredibly sexy about you when you're angry."

She glared at him as color rose up her neck. "You're an ass. And there's nothing sexy about me at all when I'm angry. And don't be thinking that saying things like that will make me less angry, because it won't."

Tyler fought the urge to laugh again and realized he did that a lot around Brooke. He relaxed in the chair and met her gaze. "Why don't you have a tree?"

She scowled. "Huh?"

"A Christmas tree," he explained. "You seem like a traditional kind of girl underneath all the swagger and bravado. So, why no tree?"

"I haven't bothered with a tree since my parents died."

"Why not?"

She sighed heavily and returned to the sofa. "I guess it's one of those times that are hard to face, like birthdays and anniversaries. Once Matt left it was as though my whole family had gone. And then when Doyle took off for Texas it just became easier to avoid celebrating things. Don't get me wrong, I have an aunt and two cousins in town who I'm really close to and my group of friends, most of whom you met. But once the core of my family was gone I just let traditions slide. It was easier, you see, to not be surrounded by the memory of what was."

Tyler understood her meaning better than she probably knew. "Your friends would walk through fire for you."

"I know," she said, nodding. "I'd do the same for them. What about you?" she asked, flipping the conversation. "What's your usual holiday routine?"

"I don't think I have one," he admitted. "Work, probably. I don't have a wife or children, or a significant other at the moment, so the holidays are usually spent with friends or with a mountain of paperwork from whatever case I'm working on."

"Why don't you?" she asked enquiringly. "Have a wife and kids. I mean, you'd be considered something of a catch in most circles... Aren't there any lady lawyers who would fit the bill?"

"None I like enough to marry," he replied, aware that the mood between them was suddenly shifting.

"Ah, we're back to that," she said, brows up. "You want to fall in *like* with someone first. I remember."

"You don't agree?"

"Not especially. Liking someone is all well and good if you want a hiking buddy or someone to carpool with... but for marriage... I think it has to be deeper than that. I think it has to be all consuming. When I get married,

I'd like him to be so crazy in love with me that he can't think straight."

Tyler saw her cheeks flush and he thought that she'd never looked more beautiful. "You're one of those sappy romantics, right?"

"I guess. But not you?"

"I've never really thought about it. I suppose I can be romantic if I need to be."

"You mean in order to get laid?" she asked bluntly.

Tyler fidgeted in his seat. He wasn't sure talking with Brooke about this subject was the best idea. "That's a somewhat cynical way of looking at it."

"Not if it's the truth. You know that old saying about how men use romance to get sex, and women use sex to get romance? Well, it's been true for a long time."

"You're probably right," he said agreeably. "I don't think it's rocket science to conclude that in general terms men and women think about sex differently."

"My point exactly. I mean, if we were both thinking about sex right now, I'm sure we'd be thinking very different things."

Tyler swallowed hard, trying to ignore his stirring libido. He wasn't so sure they would be thinking different things. For one, he was capable of seeing when a woman was attracted to him. She could deny it, but the eyes didn't lie. Which made him wonder what she would do if he got up and walked across the room and took her into his arms.

Of course, he didn't. And wouldn't. But still, he wondered if she knew how sexy, how alluring, she really was. In that moment he couldn't remember being around a more beautiful or desirable woman in his life. She wasn't coy or indecisive. She didn't seem like the kind of person who played games or manipulated situations to suit her own agenda. She possessed a kind of straightforwardness that appealed to him. That, combined with her indigo eyes, lovely curves and healthy complexion had him on the ropes. He wanted her. More than he could remember wanting anyone before.

In his arms.

In his bed.

Which meant one thing…he had to get away from her…and fast.

Chapter Seven

Brooke spent the remainder of the day either in the stables, in the kitchen or entertaining Cara. And well away from Tyler and his seductive green-eyed gaze. After their interaction in the living room, her blabbing every detail of her life and then their conversation about sex, he'd pleaded he had work to do and bailed to her small office with his laptop so he could use her internet connection and get some work done. But she wasn't fooled—he was as keen to be away from her as she was to be away from him.

She tapped on the office door at midday and said there was lunch in the kitchen but didn't hang around to share the food or his company. But she thoroughly enjoyed the time she had with her niece. Cara was such a delightfully happy child and the more time Brooke spent with her, the harder she fell. She called Matt and left a curt message. She couldn't say why he had to come home—that would be too much for him to take in. But she insisted he *had* to contact her. And finally, at four o'clock, she got a reply.

Hey, what's up?

Brooke stared at the text for a few minutes. *Oh, Matthew...everything is up.* She steeled her resolve and wrote a reply.

We need to talk. Please call me.

A few more minutes passed and then her cell beeped.

Sure. I'll give you a ring next week.

Brooke knew it was his way of avoiding contact. Five years without a conversation was a long time. He wouldn't call. He'd send an apology text and say he'd been out of service range or was busy with work or simply forgot. And usually she would forgive him. But not this time. Enough was enough. He had to make things right. For Cara's sake.

That's not good enough. If you don't call soon, don't bother to contact me ever again.

It felt harsh as she pressed the send key. But it had to be done. It was Sunday. She had days, not weeks. Friday was Christmas day. Cara's birthday. And Matthew needed to come home to claim his daughter. But she feared that if she told him there was a baby waiting for him upon his arrival, he might never come home. He'd run from trouble once before and he might do it again. She wasn't about to risk Cara's future by saying too much, too soon.

Tyler stayed out of her way for most of the day, almost as though he was giving her time alone with her niece.

Or maybe he simply didn't want to spend any more time in *her* company. Whatever his reasons, she was grateful for the opportunity to create memories with Cara. Especially since, if Tyler did take the baby back to New York, those memories would be all she had left.

At four thirty she placed the baby in the playpen in the living room with a bottle of juice and her favorite blanket and then stopped by the office to let Tyler know she was heading outside to bed down the animals for the night. She lingered in the doorway, thinking how elementally masculine and attractive he looked in those well-fitted jeans, and how way off base her first impression had been a couple of days earlier.

"Everything okay?" he inquired, clicking his laptop to a screen saver and then settling back on the office chair.

Brooke nodded. "Fine. I'll be back once the animals are fed. And I thought I'd chop some firewood. The central heating can be a little unreliable in this place, compliments of old pipes I haven't been able to afford to replace. I like to have some firewood on standby, just in case."

"Sure. But I'll chop the firewood when you get back."

She was about to debate the point, but stopped herself. She hated chopping wood and only did it out of necessity. Having it done for her was a luxury she would enjoy while it lasted. "Okay."

"What?" he queried, his mouth twisted wryly. "No argument?"

"It's my least favorite chore," she explained. "So knock yourself out. I mean, don't literally knock yourself out… but the wood and the ax are behind the stables, near the chicken run. Just be careful because the ax is sharp."

He chuckled. "Kind of has to be, to chop wood. But rest assured I'll do my best to not spill any of my city-boy blood."

"Oh," she said and rested a hand on the door frame. "I suspect there's more country in you than I first thought."

"Nebraska born and bred, remember," he said and smiled.

Brooke's insides contracted. "I guess that explains why you look so good in jeans and a cowboy hat."

He smiled. "Do you think?"

She ignored the way her skin heated. "You know, Nebraska's state line isn't too far away from here," she said, mouth curling. "You could almost drive down and see your parents for Christmas in a day if you wanted to."

His jaw tightened. "Yes, I suppose I could."

"Or you could invite them here," she suggested and wondered what kind of craziness had her offering such a thing. But she wasn't a mean-spirited person and suspected that Tyler had some lingering family issues that needed attention.

Like I do.

She ignored the stab of guilt. Considering that she'd just given her absent brother an ultimatum, she didn't really want to think about her own troubles for the moment. "There's plenty of room and it would be a chance for you to connect with your folks."

He laughed humorlessly. "You're good, you know that. Keep my mind off your brother's lack of response to your calls by inviting my parents here. I almost admire your tactics. But I have no intention of allowing my mom anywhere near here... She'd take one look at you, this small town, the baby and start sending out wedding invitations."

Brooke colored to the roots of her hair. The notion shouldn't have made her heart beat faster. But it did. His words evoked a startling picture in her head. An image she liked more than she could dare admit. "She wants to see you, um…settled, does she?"

"Don't all mothers?" he said. "Although, I think it's more about her eagerness to become a grandmother. Any way she can, I should add. I'm pretty sure she'd be delighted if I married a single mom with half a dozen kids already."

Brooke's rolling insides did a somersault. Marriage. Babies. Everything she wanted. Everything she would never have. "You want children?"

He nodded. "Of course. One day."

Her heart sank foolishly. "Surely your mom knows you'd never settle down in a small town?"

His brows came together briefly. "My mother is a romantic," he said and half smiled. "Like you. I think she believes once I meet the right woman I'll go where the heart takes me."

Her quivering insides rattled so hard she was sure he could hear. "And would you?"

"Time will tell, I suppose."

Brooke shook off the silly fantasy rolling around in her head and quickly excused herself to get her chores done.

By the time she returned to the house she'd worked off some of her stress, and headed straight for Cara, calling out to Tyler that she was bathing her niece. She heard the back door slam and assumed he'd gone outside to chop and collect the firewood. Clearly, they were intent on avoiding each other. And maybe that was for the best.

Just as the sun was setting over half an hour later, with Cara bathed, fed and put down in her crib for the night, Brooke grabbed the baby monitor and headed for the kitchen.

She was about to walk around the counter when the back door opened and Tyler swiftly framed the doorway, breathing hard, wearing the sheepskin jacket and with snowflakes in his hair. He looked so gorgeous her breath was knocked from her lungs. He didn't move. He simply stared, starting at her feet and sliding upward, up past her legs and hips, lingering on her chest for a moment, until he finally met her eyes. Brooke glanced down, realizing the T-shirt she wore left little to the imagination thanks to Cara's splashing at bath time. The damp fabric clung to her, outlining her heaving breasts and hardened nipples, making it evident she was wholly and excruciatingly aware of him in that moment. The air between them thickened and there was suddenly enough heat generated to start a bonfire.

"Brooke…"

His words trailed off, as though in that moment, he had as little control over the situation as she did. The attraction between them was undeniable. And hotter than Hades. She'd never experienced such intense desire for anyone before. It was physical and chemical rolled together. And it was out of her control.

"I should go back to the hotel," he said flatly.

Brooke's heart pounded behind her ribs. "No… I mean…why…"

"You know why," he said, not moving. "Because I'm… conflicted."

So was she, but she figured it was for a different reason than him. Brooke had only had two physical relationships in her thirty-two years. One with Doyle and the other with her high school boyfriend. After high school and before she'd met Doyle, she was too invested in her career to waste time looking for love or sex. And she had never, ever, felt the burning attraction for either of them that she did for Tyler Madden—a man she had known only two days. Two days! It was impossible. Her libido had gone haywire. It was madness. The kind of thing that happened to other women. Not to her. She was too grounded. Too sensible. She was the one her friends confided in about boyfriends and lovers. She wasn't *that* girl. She didn't get swoony. She didn't fall for guys she hardly knew.

Fall...

No. That would be crazy. Plain. Old. Stupid. Crazy. And she could never let him know it.

"You don't have to leave."

"I do," he said coolly and stepped into the room. "Because if I don't, at some point, you and I are going to end up in bed together. And I think we both know that's out of the question, considering the circumstances."

The circumstances. Cara. Matt. The whole complicated mess. And he was right...sex would muddle an already muddled situation. And she wasn't a one-night stand kind of girl.

"We won't," she said hotly. "I'm not... I'm not a casual sex kind of person. If you are and think I'll—"

"I'm not," he assured her. "Not that I live like a monk... but I don't jump from bed to bed."

She was foolishly pleased to hear it, even though it couldn't matter to her. All that mattered was that if he left, he'd take Cara with him...and that was unthinkable.

"Please," she said on a whisper, feeling emotion grip her throat like a vise. "I don't want you to go. I need this time with Cara," she admitted on a rush of breath. "If my brother doesn't come back, it might be the only time I have."

He stared at her. Deeply and intensely. He had a way of doing that like no one else ever had. And without understanding why, in that moment, Brooke let him in, right down, to the core of her soul. There were no barriers in that moment. No barricades. No defense. Just pure, raw vulnerability. And she knew he saw it all…her loneliness, her fear, her sadness. She watched as he swallowed hard, saw him nod imperceptibly, and then he spoke.

"Alright. I'll stay."

And then he walked past her, grabbed the baby monitor and left the room without another word.

Cold showers had their purpose. Even in the middle of a South Dakota winter. And this one was as cold as Tyler could stand. He stayed under the shower, absorbing the painful sting of the icy-cold needles of water on his skin, for as long as it took to get Brooke's tantalizing image out of his mind.

And failed.

Furious with himself, he switched off the faucet and grabbed a towel, quickly dried off and changed into fresh jeans and a navy Aran sweater. He stared at his opened suitcase and figured the sensible thing to do was pack his bag, collect Cara and go back to O'Sullivans while he still had the mental strength to do so. But be damned if he could get the image of Brooke's eyes out of his head. Her gaze haunted him and now made him do something that was unfamiliar territory—which was go against his own better judgment. He always trusted his instincts. He'd had to since he'd run away from home at sixteen. The streets of New York were no place for a naive teen lacking good sense and he'd grown up quickly. He'd gotten a lawyer, a job and, once he was emancipated, went back to school and then college. Over the years he'd faced his fair share of adversaries and rarely made an error in the courtroom. And he never allowed anyone to sway his sense of logic and reason.

Until today.

Until Brooke had bared herself to him in a way no one else had before. Looking into her indigo eyes had done something to him. Seeing her vulnerability had made him feel vulnerable, too.

And then he'd caved, ignoring the good sense he possessed in abundance.

He left the room to check on Cara and after he assured himself she was settled for the night, returned to the kitchen. Brooke was sitting at the table, her cell phone in her hands.

"Hey."

She looked up and sighed. "I heard from Matt."

Tyler stepped farther into the room. Her flat voice didn't sound very encouraging. "And?"

"I told him to call me."

Tyler could see the unhappiness etched in her expression. "Then I'm sure he will."

"I hope so. If he calls…if he comes back, will you stay longer? I mean, so that he can get to know her, learn to love her."

"Once I know he wants to be a father to Cara? Yes, of course I will."

She nodded a little unsteadily. "Thank you."

"Brooke, we should probably—"

"Can we not?" she asked and stood, scraping back the chair. "I already feel like the biggest fool of all time. And frankly, I don't want a postmortem about our last conversation. You made your point…and you're right. The truth is, I'm not in the market for a one-night stand and I just want to get through this week concentrating on Cara and trying to get my brother to come home. I don't do *casual*. I don't do *crazy*. And I don't think you do, either. So, whatever is going on here, I think we should both just get over it and focus on what's important…and that's the adorable little girl down the hall."

"I agree," he said quietly.

"Good," she said and pointed to the kitchen counter. "You said you could cook, right? I've left out the fixings for burritos. I'm going to hit the shower."

Tyler watched her leave the room and then he heaved a sigh of relief once she, and the scent of her shampoo, were gone. He spent the next half hour making burritos, and when she returned to the kitchen the mood between them seemed lighter than it had all day. They ate, made small talk and avoided discussing anything remotely personal. By nine o'clock the kitchen was cleaned up and Tyler was about to excuse himself when he heard Cara through the baby monitor. He checked her, changed her diaper and gave her a small bottle to send her back to sleep.

"She's such a sweet girl," Brooke said softly, standing in the doorway.

Tyler dimmed the light on the bedside table and stepped away from the crib. "Yes, she is. And incredibly resilient. Although, she misses her mom."

"She has you," Brooke said as he met her by the doorway. "You're remarkable with her. It's as if she…as if she could be yours."

"But she's not," Tyler reminded her, looking down, realizing they were close enough to touch. "I'm a temporary fixture in her life. And she needs something permanent."

Brooke nodded a little. "I know. But still, you'll make a good father one day."

A strange sensation uncurled in his belly, but he quickly dismissed it. "I hope so. If I'm lucky."

"Well…good night."

Tyler remained where he was. Because if he moved,

he knew the only thing he would do was take Brooke in his arms and kiss her beautiful mouth. "Good night."

He watched as she turned and swayed down the hall. She stopped outside her bedroom, lingering for a few seconds as their gazes met. It wasn't an invitation…it was the furthest thing from it. And yet, it felt inviting. It felt beckoning. It felt like the most natural thing in the world to take a few steps down the hallway and join her in her bedroom.

Which is why he took off for his own room, closed the door and spent the next few hours staring at the ceiling. And wondering how the hell he was supposed to get through the next few days.

He slept late and once he dragged himself out of bed and dressed, he found Cara's crib empty and then both Laughton females in the kitchen having a good time over spilled cereal and milk.

"Dada, Dada."

Cara's voice silenced anything he was about to say as the baby spotted him and held out her arms. Tyler's entire body went rigid. Brooke's head jerked around instantly and their gazes clashed. Shock worked its way through his blood. Of course, he should have expected it, since he'd spent so much time with Cara over the past few months. But still, hearing some of her first decipherable words directed toward him made him realize how attached she had become.

So have I.

Of course it was impossible not to care for the little girl. He wasn't made of stone. Maybe he did have some commitment issues—at least he did according to his last girlfriend. That didn't mean he was incapable of forming an attachment to an orphaned child. Like he'd been doing. Because he was an orphan, too.

Where did that come from?

He stopped thinking of himself as an orphan a long time ago. He had parents and they were good people. And Cara had at least one parent, even if he hadn't yet shown his face.

"She thinks you're her daddy," Brooke said, jerking him back to the present. "I'm not surprised."

Tyler ignored her comment and headed for the coffee-pot. Cara was still happily chanting "Dada" and he had to pretend it didn't mean anything. Because he wasn't Cara's father. Matthew Laughton was. He only hoped the younger man had the courage to claim what was his.

"So, what are your plans for today?" he asked evenly, grabbing a mug to pour coffee.

"I have to head into town. I should be home by one, or two at the latest. It's stopped snowing at least. Looks like it might hold off for a few days."

He nodded and muttered something about having work to do of his own, which was true enough. He had a couple of emails needing his attention and his assistant had sent him a few memos that required a response. Brooke left soon after and Tyler was ridiculously grateful for the solitude. He moved his laptop into the living room and with Cara happy to hang out in her playpen, he managed to get some much-needed work done. It was nearly one o'clock when he heard a car pull up outside and less than a minute when there was the sound of boots on the porch and a sharp rap on the front door. Cara was dozing in her pen, so he headed down the hall and opened the door. A striking-looking woman in her sixties and two men around his own age were standing behind the screen.

He searched for his manners. "Can I help you?"

The woman spoke first. "You certainly can. You're the lawyer, I presume?"

Tyler's hand rested on the door handle. "That's right."

"I'm Colleen Parker, Brooke's aunt."

Right. Now he could see the family resemblance. And the two men hovering were certainly Brooke's cousins— he'd done his research on them. One was a rancher and the other an army veteran who Brooke had told him now owned a tavern in town. He opened the door and let them cross the threshold as he introduced himself.

"Brooke isn't here," he said once the handshakes were done.

"It's my great-niece I came to see," Colleen Parker said, giving Tyler the sense that this formidable woman wouldn't take any refusal lightly.

"She's in the living room. Resting," he added, and then followed the trio down the hall.

But formidable quickly turned to mush once the older woman had Cara in her arms. He spent the following half hour answering questions and trying to respond as politely and as vaguely as he could. The two men, Grady and Brant Parker respectively, regarded him with the kind of caution he expected, considering he was now cohabitating with their much-loved cousin and held Cara's future in his hands. But they were equally polite and both very caring toward their much-younger second cousin.

"Any sign of Matt?" Grady, the older brother, asked quietly.

"Not yet," he replied.

"He was a good kid," Colleen said and smiled warmly, holding a now wide-awake Cara on her lap. "And the accident was just that…an accident. He shouldn't punish himself forever for something he didn't mean to do."

Clearly Brooke hadn't told her family about the other car involved. Which meant they probably didn't know about Pritchard and the extent of her financial troubles.

Well, he certainly had no intention of betraying her confidence.

As much as he'd appreciated the solitude when Brooke had taken off that morning, he was relieved when she returned. She strode into the house, in jeans and a bright red jacket, her hair a lovely golden halo around her shoulders. She smiled when she spotted him and the gesture eased the knot sitting in his gut. United in wanting to protect Cara, she came and sat beside him on the sofa. For a moment he thought she was going to grab his hand for support, and when she didn't he pressed his palms into his knees to avoid inadvertently touching her.

"Cara's a beautiful child," Colleen said and smiled. "And so well behaved."

Brooke laughed softly as Cara held her arms out toward her. She took the baby from Colleen and sat back on the sofa. "But you haven't seen her at bath time. She loves to splash. And at dinner time we usually end up with baby food on our clothes and in our hair," she said and hooked a thumb in Tyler's direction. "Sometimes we have to duck and weave."

As unintentional as it was, her words actually made them sound like a couple and he didn't miss the look in Colleen Parker's eyes. Brooke's aunt was obviously curious about their budding relationship.

But Brooke handled the pressure of her family's questioning with grace and patience. More than he would have granted, he was sure. Her family were nice people, perhaps a little intense and nosy, though he understood their collective concern. But Colleen, he discovered, was relentless and by the time the trio left the older woman knew where he was from, where his parents lived and the law firm he worked for. And when they discovered that Cara had a birthday on Christmas Day, they insisted it would be a double celebration.

In the course of an hour he felt like he'd been sucked into another stratosphere. Brooke's world. And he wasn't sure he wanted to leave it. Which meant one thing...he was in way deeper than he'd planned or wanted. And had no idea how to dig himself out.

One thing Brooke could always rely on—that her aunt Colleen and her two cousins would rally around and give her all the support she needed. Except, all she really wanted to do was spend some quality time with Cara and try to *not* think about how she was falling for a man she barely knew. Of course, her family would think her crazy. And they would be right. It was foolish to waste energy thinking about Tyler in *that* way. He'd made his intentions clear—see Cara reunited with Matt, and if not, head back to New York with the baby and find her a nice adoptive home. Just the thought made Brooke ache inside.

Once they were gone she hauled Cara into her arms and headed for the kitchen to make coffee for herself and a bottle for the baby. Tyler returned to the office and spent ten or so minutes there before joining them in the kitchen.

"You were grilled," she said, more as a statement than question. "Sorry about that."

"Don't be," he replied easily. "Your family are nice people. And they clearly love the idea of having Cara in their lives."

"Who wouldn't," she said as she nestled the toddler against her hip. "This little girl is easy to love."

"True. Tell me something. Why haven't you told your family the truth about the accident? And about the other car involved?"

She shrugged. "A few reasons. For Matt, mostly. This

is a small town and Frank Pritchard is a powerful man here. It was so long ago and I really don't want the whole business stirred up again. Besides, once I say one thing, it will lead to another and then another. And I don't want sympathy or have my family trying to help me out financially."

"Which they would obviously do," he said and raised one brow. "Right?"

"Sure," she replied. "Grady and Brant would help me in a heartbeat. But I won't take any handouts."

He rocked back a little on his heels. "Whoa...there's that pride again, stopping you from being practical."

Brooke ignored the heat sliding over her skin. How she could want him and be so mad at his condescending arrogance simultaneously, made her blood boil. She put Cara in the high chair and walked around the countertop, shoulders back. "My pride. My business."

"They're family. Maybe it's time to be less proud and more flexible."

"I'm plenty flexible," she said, and for a flash of a second had an image of being so flexible she had her legs wrapped around his hips. "Incidentally, this is a bit rich coming from someone who is probably the most arrogant know-it-all I've ever met. Someone who divorced his parents, works seventy-hour weeks and spends the holidays alone."

He laughed and the sound warmed her down to her toes. "Bravo. Did it feel good to get that off your chest?"

"Yes," she admitted. "Very good. Cathartic, in fact. And very satisfying."

As soon as she said the words Brooke knew she shouldn't have. The sudden gleam in his eyes spoke volumes and the heat in her cheeks amplified immediately.

"Well," he said, crossing his arms as he rested his behind against the counter, "I'm glad I can satisfy you in some ways, if not others."

Oh, sweet heaven...dig me a great big hole right now so I can hide from this.

But none came. Instead she plastered a smile on her face so fake it made her jaw ache. "By the way," she said, meeting his gaze, "I didn't mean to make you uncomfortable this morning. When Cara called you her... you know."

"You didn't," he said, not moving. "I should have expected it. We've spent a lot of time together recently and it's natural that she would think that. But I don't want to confuse her, particularly if your brother shows up and accepts his responsibility."

Brooke kept her gaze steady. "I know what you said you'd do if Matt doesn't come home," she said, her heart breaking just a little with every word. "But have you considered adopting her yourself?"

He suddenly looked like he was etched in stone. "No."

"Why not?" she asked quietly. "I mean, you're great with her and she clearly adores you."

"Because she needs a family," he said firmly. "A mom and dad who—"

"She needs someone to love her," Brooke said, glancing at the baby as she cooed and played with the sippy cup in her hands. "And you do, as much as you want to deny it."

"I'm not denying it," he said. "I care for her a great deal. But I'm not in a position to be a parent. I'm not married and I work long hours." He pushed himself up and walked around the counter, turning to face her, hands on hips. "And frankly, I find your suggestion highly irregular, considering you've been adamant that she belongs here, with you."

Brooke clutched the edge of the counter. "Of course I want her here. But if that can't happen—if you can't find it in your heart to leave her here even if Matt doesn't return, then I would prefer that she be with someone I know. Someone I...trust."

Someone I like.

Someone I more than like.

She almost passed out the moment the thought entered her head. It was ridiculous. People didn't start falling in love in two days. It was physical attraction. It was desire and lust and everything that had to do with her libido, and nothing to do with her heart.

How can I be falling in love with someone I haven't touched? Someone I haven't kissed? Someone I haven't made love with? Someone who is the polar opposite of me in every way?

And yet, deep down, she suspected they *were* alike in a lot of ways. He had integrity. He was respectful and considerate. He was a good listener. Qualities she'd always endeavored to have herself.

Yes, Tyler Madden *was* the type of man she could fall in love with.

And even though she knew it was foolish, Brooke knew she was already halfway there.

Chapter Eight

"So," Kayla said as she stirred her coffee. "How are things going with that lawyer you're shacked up with?"

Brooke scowled and ignored the wicked gleam in her friend's eyes. "Fine."

They were at The Muffin Box café on Wednesday morning, having a quick catch-up over coffee and cake and talking about Lucy Monero's recent engagement to Brooke's cousin Brant and the upcoming wedding.

Ash offered a gentle nod. "Are you sure? You look a little far away."

"I'm right here. And I'm good, I promise."

But she hated lying to her friends. She wasn't good. She wasn't even remotely okay. The last couple of days had been some of the hardest of her life. With no word from Matt, and with Brooke getting more attached to Cara each day—plus her attraction for Tyler seeming to have a will of its own—things had never been more complicated. And there was the financial mess hanging over her head. But she also didn't want to dissect her life with the other women. Oh, they'd understand, and they'd offer sympathy and reassuring words...but she wasn't in the mood for pity or compassion. Not even from three people she cared about.

"Any word from Matt?" Lucy asked.

She shook her head. "Not yet."

"When does Pretty Boy leave?" Kayla asked, grinning.

"Don't call him that," Brooke said firmly and pushed a fork through her raspberry muffin.

The three women were instantly silent. In the end it was Ash who spoke first. "Brooke...is something going on between you two?"

"No," she replied honestly. "Not...exactly."

"Do you mean *not yet*?" Kayla, always the frankest of the group, asked.

"It's complicated."

"Sex generally is," Lucy said and smiled. "Whether you're having it or not."

"Well," she said, mortified that she was actually having the conversation. "We're not. I like him, okay," she admitted. "He's successful and handsome and charming and single, so of course I like him. I'm only human. I may have been off the dating scene for the past couple of years, but I haven't been in a coma."

The trio laughed and Kayla spoke next. "Off the dating scene?" she echoed. "Seriously? Is that what you'd call it?"

"Sure," Brooke replied and grinned sweetly. "How is Liam O'Sullivan, by the way?"

Kayla rolled her eyes. "Nice try. But we're talking about you today."

"No, we're not," Brooke said as she pushed the barely touched muffin aside, "because I have to bail. I just came into town for a doctor's appointment and need to get back. I'd like to spend as much time with Cara as I can while she's here. And since my brother hasn't shown up or called, I may only have a few more days to enjoy being an aunt."

Or a mother.

She didn't say it. But she knew her friends would be thinking the same thing. They all knew about her fertility issues and long battle with crippling endometriosis that ended with several surgeries and a load of heartache. They all knew she would never be a mother. Brooke had resigned herself to the fact years ago, but being around Cara had awakened something inside her and now, more than ever before, made her mourn what she would never have. But she would never show it, never let anyone witness her grief. She'd made that mistake with Doyle and he'd trampled all over her feelings. It was better kept inside. Safe. Hidden. Forgotten.

When she got back to the ranch she was surprised to see that Tyler's rental car was missing. For a few anxious seconds she thought that perhaps he'd packed up his things and Cara and left. But after a quick scout around the house she spotted Cara's playpen, high chair and her favorite toys scattered around the living room. Plus, deep down she knew Tyler wouldn't be so clandestine. He'd promised her a week and he wouldn't go back on his word.

He returned after lunch while Brooke was in the kitchen going over a few household accounts. Cara was clearly delighted to see her and immediately begged to be cuddled. Brooke obliged and scooped her out of Tyler's arms.

"Did you have a nice time with your friends?" he asked and placed a grocery bag on the counter.

"Yes, thank you. What's this?" She peered into the bag.

"It's my turn to cook," he said and grinned. "Risotto."

"You can cook risotto? I'm impressed."

"Well, wait until you taste it before you pass judgment."

"Okay," she promised, smiling. "So, where did you get to today?"

He pulled the groceries from the bag. "I had a few errands to run, and then I bumped into your aunt while I was in town. Colleen insisted on watching over Cara for an hour while I caught up on a few things."

"Oh," she said, feeling a little disappointed. "I would have stayed home and looked after her myself if I'd known you were heading out. I could have easily changed my doctor's appointment."

He frowned. "You went to the doctor? Is everything alright?"

"Yes," she replied. "Just a routine checkup." She looked at him, thinking how domestic the whole scene was. He was easy to be around. Easy to like. Easy to love, for that matter. Brooke pushed the notion from her thoughts and spoke again. "Since the snow has eased off I thought we might take her for a walk in the stroller."

"I'm not sure the stroller will get through the slush on the ground. But I can carry her," he suggested.

"I think I'll grab a thermos and a few snacks," she said, smiling. "We may as well make an afternoon of it. You get her diaper bag and rig her up and I'll meet you back here in fifteen minutes."

Three hours later they were still out hiking. Cara was fast asleep against Tyler's shoulder as they walked the fence line before heading down toward the river. The spruce trees were covered in a blanket of snow and Brooke pointed out some of the birds unique to the area.

He came to a halt and looked out over the river. "It's a beautiful spot, Brooke. I can see why you want to fight so fiercely to protect it."

She sucked in a long gulp of crisp air. "I couldn't imagine living anywhere else. Even when I was on the road, going from competition to competition, living in the back of a horse trailer or spending the night in a crappy motel, I always felt that no matter where I went, home was always here, waiting for me to return."

"Until tragedy forced you back permanently."

Heat clung to her throat. She knew he could feel how important the land was to her, and how much it cost her emotionally when she lost her parents and Brooke wasn't about to deny it.

"I miss them every day," she admitted. "And I miss Matt, too. I miss my goofy little brother who always made me laugh. He's a good person, Tyler. Sure, he was a bit wayward when he was a teenager and did a few foolish things. But who hasn't been foolish once or twice in their life? I know I have."

"Really?" he queried, looking at her as he gently held Cara's head. "I can't imagine you doing anything foolish. You seem too sensible for that."

Brooke smiled. "I'm not always sensible. Proud and unbendable, remember?"

"You're just protecting what's yours the best way you can," he said quietly. "It's not so hard to understand."

Her eyes burned. "Would you stop that?"

"Stop what?"

"Being so...nice."

He grinned. "But I'm a nice guy."

"I know," she said and walked a few steps through the melting snow. "That's what terrifies me."

He caught up in a few strides. "I told you that first

night that I'm not a threat to you. I mean it. I know it might seem that way, considering I might have to leave with Cara. But it's not...personal, you know. It's not about you. It's this situation, that's all. Honestly, I think you're incredible. And strong. And resilient. And...quite beautiful."

Her entire body stilled. It was easily the sweetest thing anyone had ever said to her. "You see, you *are* nice. And I'm...vulnerable to that, as it turns out."

She walked off again, breathless from the cold air and the feelings running riot through her system. Brooke pulled the beanie further down over her ears and kept walking, mindful that he was only a few steps behind her. Even though he carried Cara, the diaper bag and the small knapsack she'd filled with a coffee thermos and a few snacks, he could easily keep up with her. But he let her have her space. He seemed to know what she needed. And it made Brooke fall for him even more.

By the time they got back to the ranch she was exhausted. But she had animals to attend to and used that as an excuse to be alone for a while. She stayed outside until half past five o'clock and when she entered the house through the mudroom, she could smell dinner cooking and realized Cara was already fed and bathed and in her crib.

"She was beat," he said when she glanced at the empty high chair. "I think we wore her out."

"She's not the only one," Brooke remarked and pulled off her beanie and scarf. "I'm going to take a shower. Be back soon." She got to the door and turned. "That smells great, by the way. You really are good at everything."

It wasn't meant to sound sarcastic. It was simply a statement of fact. She'd bet her boots whatever he touched turned out well. Brooke left the room swiftly and headed for the shower. The warm water eased the tension clutching the back of her neck and when she was done she dried herself off and then dressed in a long denim skirt, red blouse and a pair of low-heeled boots. She brushed her hair and stared at her reflection in the bathroom mirror.

What did Tyler see, she wondered, when he looked at her? Did he see freckles and a chin that was a little too square to be considered truly feminine? Did he see a mouth that was wider than what was fashionable? Or a nose that was cute at best and hair that had a will of its own when left out? Put together she figured she didn't look too bad…not girl-next-door pretty like Lucy or movie-star beautiful like Kayla. Attractive…passable. A face that wouldn't exactly stand out in a crowd. But one that looked earnest and honest and real.

With a sigh, she fluffed her hair with her fingertips and headed back to the kitchen.

Dinner was delicious and the conversation flowed. By the time the dishes were being done she realized again how easy Tyler was to be around. Almost a week into their acquaintance and her estimation of him had altered dramatically. Sure, he had an arrogant streak and liked to give his opinion freely. But he was also kind and thoughtful and possessed a kind of inner strength she almost envied. He would be a good role model for Matt, she thought, if her brother ever bothered to call or show up. In a few days Tyler would be leaving and he would take Cara with him. If Matt didn't make contact soon, she might lose her niece forever.

"Everything okay?" he asked, almost as if he'd sensed the shift in her mood.

They were in the living room, sitting in opposite chairs, a mile away from one another, drinking soda. And yet,

Brooke felt his nearness like it were a blanket, warm and protective and exactly what she craved.

"Sure," she said and faked a smile. "Just feeling a touch melancholy."

"It's that time of year," he said, watching her over the rim of his glass. "You know, we can get a tree tomorrow if you want. I saw a place in town this morning that was selling them. Cara would probably like it."

Brooke's brows rose slowly. "Cara? Or you?"

He shrugged a little. "I'm feeling less like a Grinch this year."

She grinned. "I'm glad to hear it. Especially since we've agreed to spend Christmas afternoon at my aunt's—and she is really into the whole festive thing."

"Do I need to buy gifts?"

Brooke shook her head. "No. We only buy for the kids now and I've got that covered. It's really a day to eat to excess and lounge around Grady's ranch house and watch football." She smiled and met his gaze. "You like football, right?"

"I'm from New York," he said, as though that was enough, and then grinned. "And I have season tickets to the Giants."

Brooke laughed. "Then I'm sure you will fit right in."

"Did your ex-fiancé fit right in?" he asked unexpectedly.

He wanted to know about Doyle? Brooke frowned a little. "Um... I guess. He was a cowboy. Friendly, charming... you know the type."

"The type that leaves his fiancée for another woman."

Brooke's chin came up. "He left me to be with his son. Once I got past the hurt, I understood. He wanted to be with his child. That's a strong bond to ignore."

"For some. For others, not so much."

Brooke heard the tinge of resentment in his voice and pressed a little more. "Like your birth parents?"

He shrugged. "I have to believe that they did what they thought was right at the time. And I'm grateful for the parents that I do have," he said and met the query in her gaze. "Despite how it might seem."

She drew in a steadying breath. "It must have hurt them…what you did. Running away and filing for emancipation. Do you regret it?"

"Yes," he replied flatly. "In part. But, you know that old expression about not being able to put an old head on young shoulders…at the time I felt as though it was my only option. Otherwise they would have dragged me back to Nebraska."

"And yet, here you are," she said softly. "Just over the border."

Tyler got to his feet abruptly and moved around the room, coming to stop at the fireplace. He touched one of the framed photographs. "If you're trying to make me feel bad about the way I have treated my parents in the past, then you're succeeding."

Guilt pressed down on her rib cage. "That wasn't my intention." Brooke got up and moved around the sofa to stand beside him. "I'm sorry."

He turned to face her, one hand resting on the mantel. "You're right, though," he said softly. "I did hurt my parents. My mom…" He stopped, his words trailing, as though they were some of the hardest he'd ever said. "My mom blamed herself and my father begged me not to go. I'd left a note and promised to call when I got to the city. When I got to New York I ended up at a youth shelter and that's how I met Ralph Jürgens. He worked out pretty quick that I was a runaway and made me call my parents. My mom was so upset she couldn't talk. And my father... he...was crying. Sobbing, really. I still remember how that made me feel...guilty and angry at the same time. Sure, they'd always been a little alternative, even before they moved in with the tree huggers. Dad drove this old jalopy that ran on biofuel and recycled everything. But he'd always been strong...solid."

"And you didn't go back?"

He shook his head. "I couldn't. I was young and arrogant and resentful of the life they'd chosen. Before I left..." Tyler looked away and swallowed. "I told them I wished they'd never adopted me."

Brooke felt his pain in his words right through to her bones and she reached out, grasping his biceps. "They must know you didn't mean it."

He nodded fractionally. "But I meant it at the time."

"You were young and overwhelmed by a lot of mixed emotions. And I can't imagine they'd be anything other than very proud of the man you have become. And they are part of that," she said, feeling the muscles beneath her palm clench. "They raised you, nurtured you, instilled the moral compass and integrity you possess by the bucket load...how could they be anything but proud?"

He looked down to where her hand lay and covered her hand with his own, linking their fingers in a way that was impossibly intimate. Palm to palm, Brooke felt the connection through her entire body. She met his eyes, saw his gaze move over her face and then focus on her mouth. Her lips parted instinctively and she sucked in a shallow breath. This energy had been building between them for days, brewing like an electrical storm. And Brooke wanted his kiss more than she had ever wanted anything or anyone in her life.

* * *

Tyler had enough experience with women to know that he was about to step into another reality with Brooke. Talking with her had unlocked something inside him… old feelings…old regrets…and made him admit things he'd never said to anyone else, ever. Talking about his personal life had always been off-limits. Not even his closest friends back in New York knew much about his upbringing and his parents. But Brooke had the ability to draw it out of him without effort. She listened. She understood.

And he wanted her.

He wanted to feel her against him, breast to chest, hip to hip, thigh to thigh.

Reaching around, he cupped the back of her neck, tilting her head back slightly. Her lips were apart, inviting him, and he bent his head and touched them with his own. Sensation rocked through him, climbing over his skin and through his blood. Her mouth opened beneath his and her free hand moved around his waist. She was close, pressing against him, and he leaned in closer still. Finesse and resistance flew out the window as Tyler deepened the kiss, finding her tongue and rolling it around his own. She tasted so good, like raspberry soda and peppermints. And she was soft and luscious and her curves fit against him as though they were two halves of the same whole.

The kiss went on, deeper, harder, then softer, asking not taking. She didn't pull back. She kept pace with him each time he angled her head, each time he pressed closer, each time he moved his tongue against hers in an erotic slide that fueled his libido like a drug.

Finally, Tyler pulled back, breaking the kiss, staring into her upturned face.

She was all indigo eyes, all raspy breath. Her chest rose up and down, emphasizing her full breasts, and his palms itched to touch her there, to peel off her clothes and lay her bare so he could worship her breasts with his hands and mouth. And more. So he could make love to every inch of her, discovering what she liked, what would make her quiver, what would make her say his name on a sigh as she came apart in his arms.

"I want you," he said, breathless, keeping her close, trailing his mouth down her cheek to her jaw and then the sensitive skin below her ear. He pulled back again and met her gaze. "So much."

"I want you, too."

Tyler's insides constricted. "Let me make love to you tonight."

Her eyes darkened in a kind of sexy haze. "Yes," she whispered.

He grabbed her hand and pressed a kiss to her knuckles. "You're sure?"

"Positive," she said and smiled.

Tyler took a step, planning on taking Brooke with him up the hall and into his bedroom. Except a sound distracted him. The baby monitor. Cara. And she was crying.

Brooke untangled their fingers. "That doesn't sound good."

"No," he agreed. "It doesn't."

Within seconds they were both out of the room and striding up the hall. Once they reached Cara's room, Tyler turned up the night-light. Cara was sitting in her crib, clearly distressed, rubbing her eyes with small fists as she wailed. Brooke was by the crib before him and hauled the baby into her arms.

"She might need changing," she said and headed for the change table.

One diaper change later and Cara was still inconsolable. Tyler checked for a temperature but she wasn't overly warm. He used the infant thermometer to ensure she wasn't running a fever.

"Temperature is normal," he said and waited while Brooke put her into a fresh pair of pajamas. "Tummy troubles maybe. Or teething."

Brooke nodded and seemed to be working with some kind of built-in maternal instinct as she held Cara to her chest and patted the baby's back soothingly. Cara settled a little, only to start crying again when Brooke tried to put her back in the crib.

Tyler headed for the kitchen and fixed a bottle with a small amount of tepid water and when he returned to the bedroom, he found Brooke sitting on a chair in the corner, rocking the baby as she sung softly. She had a nice voice, he thought. Soft and mellow and for a while it helped Cara settle down. But it was a rough few hours that followed. Cara was upset, crying in between jabbering, and clearly not happy with the world. They took turns holding her and trying to get her back to sleep. By one o'clock, Cara finally fell asleep on his chest. The chair wasn't all that comfortable, but he stayed where he was until he was certain she wasn't going to wake up. Brooke stayed by the crib for a while, rubbing Cara's head gently when she stirred.

It was close to two before they finally turned down the night-light and moved from the room. Brooke rested her back against the wall and let out a long breath.

"Poor little thing," she said wearily. "I'm sure it's teething. I'll call my friend Lucy in the morning. She's a doctor and will know what to do. The soothing gel seemed to help a little."

He nodded. "We should try and get some sleep. I'll keep the monitor in my room."

His room. Her room. A few hours ago they were about to make love. That plan had certainly been aborted once Cara needed their attention. It was probably for the best. They hardly knew one another. Becoming friends was hard enough. Being Brooke's lover would change everything.

"Tyler, I—"

"It's better this way," he said quietly. "In the long run. Better that we don't do something foolish. Not that being with you would be anything other than incredible. But sex always—"

"Complicates things," she said, finishing his sentence. "Yes, I know. Okay," she said and pushed herself off the wall. "I'm going to bed. Alone…because that's the sensible thing to do, and I am nothing if not a sensible woman. But wake me if she stirs again. I don't mind doing my share."

Tyler nodded vaguely and headed to his room. Alone. And strangely, lonelier than he could ever remember being in his life.

Cara woke up again around five and once he got to her crib Brooke was a few seconds behind him. She wore knitted cotton pajamas with ducks on them and even in his bleary-eyed state he was achingly aware of her curves. They gave the baby a drink, a diaper change and applied some gel to her gums, and that seemed enough to get her back to sleep.

"Coffee?" Brooke suggested once the baby was back in the crib.

"Sure. I don't think I could sleep now anyhow."

"Me, either." She padded down the hall on her socked feet and returned to her room for a second, coming out with a robe in her hands. She shouldered into the garment and belted it around her waist. "Aren't you cold?"

she asked, sliding her gaze over him, taking in the navy sweatpants and white tank shirt.

He wasn't. The way her eyes raked over him was enough to keep his blood at ten thousand degrees. But he took her point and grabbed a sweater before he headed for the kitchen. Once they were settled on opposite sides of the kitchen table she let out a weary sigh.

"You know, I've done my fair share of babysitting Grady's kids over the years, but tonight was different. It was like...like..."

"Like being a parent?" he finished for her, understanding what she meant. "You mean the worry and the sense of helplessness? Yeah... I know what you mean."

"I hated seeing Cara so distressed," she said, eyes glistening a little before she blinked a couple of times. "I could actually *feel* what she was going through," Brooke said softly and tapped a hand to her heart. "In here. I never thought I'd ever experience that."

Tyler drank some coffee and looked at her over the mug. "Because you don't have children? But you're young," he remarked and watched her jaw tense. "You still have time to have a family of your own."

She dropped her gaze and stared into her coffee for a moment, then looked up and shrugged. "For now all I care about is saving my ranch and getting Matt to come home."

It seemed an odd reply, but he didn't press the issue. "Still no call from your brother?"

She shook her head. "I'm worried, Tyler. I'm worried that he's either in trouble and can't call...or he's still so wrapped up in the past that he won't call because it means he'll have to embrace the present." She took a long breath. "The truth is, I haven't told him *why* I need to speak with him," she admitted. "Maybe if I had, he'd be more inclined to reply. I just didn't want to have him make the decision to return, or not, over the telephone."

Tyler placed his mug on the table and linked his hands together. "Thank you for telling me the truth. I know this must be hard for you, Brooke. I know you're torn between doing what is right for Cara, and being loyal to your brother."

"Losing her is going to break my heart."

Tyler's throat tightened. Seeing Brooke unhappy was hard to take. The hardest thing. "I know."

And knowing he would be the one breaking her heart, just about broke his own in two.

Chapter Nine

Cara got the all clear by the doctor later that morning, much to Brooke's relief. She *was* teething and Lucy gave them instructions on how to relieve the soreness. Thankfully, the ER was quiet and they were equally thankful that Lucy was available to see to Cara's needs.

Brooke hung back to speak with her friend when Tyler picked up Cara and walked her up and down the hall to keep her occupied.

"That is one cute baby," Lucy said and smiled. "No wonder you're smitten."

Brooke nodded. "Yes, she's adorable."

"And as for that tall drink of water over there," Lucy said, dropping her voice, "I can see why you're smitten in that department, too."

Brooke colored instantly and hugged her coat around herself. "I'm not," she denied hotly.

"You *so* are."

Brooke jabbed her friend in the ribs playfully. Lucy was the most discreet person she knew. Anything she said would remain in confidence. "Okay…so maybe I am just a little."

Lucy's expression softened. "I hope it works out. If anyone deserves a happy ending, it's you."

It was a nice fantasy. Looking at Tyler as he patiently strode up and down the hall with the baby in his arms, it made the perfect picture. It was everything she'd ever wanted. A family. Of her own. Forever.

Yes…a fantasy. A teaser for a life she would never have. A daydream.

But looking at Lucy, she had to believe that dreams did sometimes come true. Her friend had been in love with Brant Parker since high school and despite the obstacles along the way, they had somehow managed to find one another, to fall in love and plan a life together.

She hugged her friend and smiled. "I'll see you tomorrow."

By the time she caught up with Tyler she was filled with emotion and silently cursing herself. She'd never been the sort of person who wept or fell in a heap. She was as tough as an old boot. Resilient and strong, that's what Tyler had called her. But the past few days had been a roller coaster and she was feeling the stress. Time was running out for Matt to make contact, Cara would almost certainly be taken back to New York if her brother didn't show up and Brooke was falling in love with a man she had known less than a week. But who seemed more familiar to her than anyone she had ever known.

They'd kissed. They'd almost made love. She could barely think about it without losing her mind. Kissing Tyler had been sweetly erotic and mind-blowing. And something else. Like…earth and rain and fire. Like coming home.

"Hey," he said, jerking her back to the present. "You look far away."

"I'm right here," she said and laughed when Cara grabbed her hand. "I'd like to go shopping and get a few things for Cara for her birthday, if that's okay? And then we could have lunch while we're in town. Unless you have other plans?"

He shook his head. "No plans. I'm all yours," he said, and she caught a gleam in his eyes. "We're all yours," he said and bounced Cara, making the baby squeal with delight.

The trouble was, Brooke wished they *were* hers.

"How about the restaurant at O'Sullivans? It's posh and pricey, so I guess you're buying," she added and laughed as they made their way out of the emergency ward.

"It would be my pleasure."

There was a boutique in town that carried a selection of baby clothes and Brooke picked out a few things for Cara and when they were done Tyler stowed the bags in the car. Then they headed out for lunch. O'Sullivans was popular because the chef, Abby Perkins, was Paris trained and well liked around town. They were seated without hassle and the waitress brought out a high chair for Cara. Liam O'Sullivan passed their table and nodded cordially.

"He seems like an intense kind of guy," Tyler remarked, half smiling.

Brooke's eyes widened. "Oh, he's one of those judgmental, know-it-all jerks."

"Just your type, then?"

She laughed and it felt good. Despite everything, despite the kisses and aborted lovemaking, it was still ridiculously easy to be around Tyler. "He's involved with my friend Kayla. So, no, not for me. I'd prefer *not* to be with a man who's in love with someone else."

"I don't think that will happen," he said so quietly she leaned in closer. "I think the man who falls in love with you will want only you, and nothing else."

Nothing else. Like no babies. No family. For a while she'd believed Doyle was that man. He'd certainly played the part, insisting it didn't matter that they would never have children. She felt safe, cherished, loved for *who* she was, and not for her barren womb. His departure had taught her not to dream about having a happily-ever-after. It wasn't fair of her to expect any man to give up his dream of fatherhood because she was unable to give him a child.

She shrugged, feeling hurt through to her bones. Cara started chatting and waving her arms and Brooke's attention was quickly diverted. It seemed *dada* was now her favorite word and she said it at every opportunity. Tyler had clearly become used to it, and although he didn't encourage the baby, he remained as attentive as always. They stayed for an hour and before they headed home Brooke mentioned she had to stop by the feed store to collect some supplements that she'd ordered for the horses. Tyler nodded, saying he needed to pick up more diapers and formula, so Brooke said she'd walk and meet him at the feed store in fifteen minutes. Once the check was settled, she kissed Cara goodbye and lingered for a moment, watching as he effortlessly strapped the baby into the backseat, waved to her where she stood on the sidewalk, and drove down the next block to the drugstore. He was so good with the baby that it made her heart ache. One day, some lucky woman would get to have his child.

But that won't be me.

She turned and began the walk toward the feed store

on Olsen Street, one block east of Main Street. It had stopped snowing and the ploughs were out in force, clearing the roads and sidewalks.

When she walked across the parking area at the front of the feed store she noticed a truck from the Pritchard Ranch parked out front. Will Serrato was at the reception counter, talking to the clerk. He nodded agreeably when he saw her and tilted his hat as always.

"Hey, Brooke. We've just been by your place."

She frowned. "We?"

"That would mean me," a voice said from behind her.

She turned to face Frank Pritchard. In his mid-sixties, he was a tall, stockily built man with a shock of auburn hair and a ruddy complexion. He also had an air of self-entitlement, as though he believed he had the right to say and do whatever he pleased whenever he liked.

"Frank…hello."

Pritchard wasn't someone who dispensed pleasantries. "You can call off the hounds now."

"Hounds?"

He scowled, wrinkling his face up. "Don't act innocent. And tell that useless attorney of yours that threats may have worked this time, but he gets one shot only."

Tension cramped her shoulders. "I have no idea what you're talking about."

His mouth twisted mockingly. "Sure you do. I don't know what he thinks he knows, or what you've said, but making veiled accusations isn't going to change the past."

The past. The accident. Her lawyer knew the details, but he'd also suggested caution when dealing with the Pritchards. Werner wasn't known for having an attack-dog style.

"I haven't said anything," she assured him.

He grunted. "Here," he said, thrusting a large envelope

into her hands. "What you wanted. It's a onetime offer. No more negotiations. Take it and sign it and get it back to your lawyer," he said and stepped back. "Or leave it. You've got seven days to make a decision. After that I ain't wasting any more time on this."

He walked off, puffing, clearly angry and Brooke stared at the envelope in her hands.

"It's a good offer, Brooke."

She looked sideways and noticed Will Serrato was still standing by the counter. The tall, good-looking cowboy was regarding her kindly. She opened the envelope and pulled out the documents inside. She scanned the pages quickly. It was an offer for the small slice of her land that Pritchard wanted. And it was generous. Very generous. Overly generous. More than the land was worth and much more than she'd ever imagined. Enough to pay the bank and have some left over. Enough to alter everything.

"I don't understand," she said, waving the papers. "What changed?"

Will shrugged loosely. "Your attorney, Stewart, came out to the ranch yesterday afternoon. He made a counter-offer and Frank accepted."

"I didn't instruct Werner to make a counteroffer."

Will's mouth twisted. "Maybe he's a better attorney than anyone gives him credit for. He sure acted like he knew what he was doing."

Suspicion climbed further up her spine. "I see." She shoved the envelope in her coat, grabbed her parcel and turned. "Thanks, Will."

Brooke spotted Tyler's rental car as soon as she hit the parking lot and headed for it. The warm air from the heater hit her the moment she slipped into the passenger seat and strapped into her seat belt. Cara was cooing in the back, Tyler looked relaxed and very pleased with himself.

Which increased her suspicions tenfold.

"Everything okay?" he asked as he eased the vehicle into Reverse. "Did you get what you needed?"

"And more," she replied cryptically.

He nodded. "I ordered a tree," he said, infuriating her more with each passing second. "It'll get dropped off at the ranch within the hour, so we should get going."

A tree? She suspected that wasn't all he'd been doing. But she wasn't about to have a discussion about it while they were on the road. "Great," she said, extra sweetly. "Let's go."

Tyler knew enough about women—and about Brooke in particular—to work out that she was furious with him about something. And given that he'd spotted the truck from the Pritchard Ranch outside the feed store, it had to have something to do with that.

He wasn't sure what she knew, and he wasn't about to deny anything.

But by the time they reached the ranch house there was so much tension in the air it could have been sliced with a knife. She hadn't spared him more than half a dozen words the entire trip back.

Brooke got out and went to Cara before he had a chance to open the car's rear door. She took the baby and headed for the house. She gave Cara a fruit snack and then put her down for a nap and over the next hour and a half there was more silence…too much of it. The tree arrived and he dragged it into the living room while she pulled a box of old decorations from the spare room. And still she hardly spoke.

"Something on your mind?" he asked as he repositioned the tree in the corner.

Her head snapped around and she glared at him. Oh, yeah…she was mad. She left the room, shoulders back, chin at a hard tilt. When she returned she had a large envelope in her hands. She dropped it onto the coffee table and thrust her hands on her hips.

"So, are you the hounds?"

Tyler stretched to his full height and glanced at the envelope. "What?"

"Take a look," she offered coolly.

He grabbed the envelope and pulled out the contents, scanning the pages briefly. "It's a good offer."

"A good offer?" she echoed, cheeks now blazing. "Are you kidding? It's an amazing offer. And it's more than the land is worth."

"He obviously wants it badly enough to set the price," Tyler said and placed the envelope back on the table. "You should take it."

Her eyes flared. "Should I? And you didn't answer my question."

"What question?"

"Are you the hounds that Pritchard referred to when he gave me this earlier? He said I could call off the hounds now. So, are you?"

Tyler folded his arms. "What do you want to know?"

"I want to know if you had a hand in this," she said. "And I want to know how you did it."

"Yes," he replied bluntly. "I did. I spoke to your attorney yesterday."

She drew in a deep breath, chin at an angle, eyes flashing fire. "You said you had errands to do and that's why you left Cara with my aunt."

"I did," he said flatly. "One errand—a meeting with

your ineffective lawyer, who now understands that he actually works for you, and not the other way around."

"You had no right."

Guilt niggled between his shoulders. "You needed help."

"But I didn't ask for it," she snapped. "Nor did I want it."

"Because you're proud and stubborn," he said, not moving. "And once you get past being angry with me, you'll see that you got a good outcome."

She shook her head. "Can you actually hear yourself? Do you not see how wrong this is?"

Irritation stirred through his blood. She *was* proud and stubborn. And he wanted to help her. Tyler wasn't about to apologize for doing what he thought was right. "It's not wrong to want to help a friend."

The thunder in her expression was relentless. "We're not friends," she snapped back. "We're not anything!"

Her words rocked him back on his heels. "No?" he queried, brows up.

Her cheeks were spotted with color and it made her freckles stand out even more. He fought the urge to stride across the room and kiss her again. But figured she'd probably slug him instead.

"One kiss doesn't make us anything. And you had no right to interfere in my private business. If I wanted help, I would have asked for it."

"But that's just it Brooke, you don't ask," he said, so calmly he knew he would only fuel her anger toward him. "You don't ask it of your family, or your friends. You've been holed up in this house for so long with only your pride for company you've forgotten what it is to ask for help, even when you need it."

"It's not your job to tell me what I need," she said,

clearly exasperated. "But you're so full of yourself you can't see past your own arrogance. I demand to know what you said to my attorney."

"I gave him some advice," he said, ignoring her insult.

"Advice?"

"Yes, advice on how to actually *be* an attorney. Or a good one, at least. I told him to present this counter-offer to Pritchard, and let him know that if he wanted to play games he would be playing them with a New York law firm."

"So, you lied?"

"Not at all. I told you I did pro bono work. I'd happily be your attorney to get you a deal that is fair and equitable."

"I have an attorney," she reminded him. "And he might not wear handmade Italian suits or have a law degree from some big-city college, but he's the person I *choose* to represent me. And you have no right to undermine that and betray me."

Tyler felt her pain right through to his bones. "It wasn't my intention to betray or hurt you. On the contrary, I only wanted to help you. You were about to lose your ranch and there was something I could do to help. I'm a lawyer... I fix problems."

"Except that I'm not *your* problem."

Okay...so perhaps he had overstepped the boundaries of their relationship. He'd gone to see her lawyer and after speaking less than half a dozen words with the other man, realized that if he didn't do something, she would lose the ranch that she loved. So, he'd done it with the best intentions. "You're overreacting," he said, impatiently running a hand through his hair. "Take Pritchard's offer, Brooke. It's good. It's solid. And it will help you get the ranch back on its feet. Maybe you can now buy that colt you want to restart your breeding program. Stay angry at me if you must…but don't let *that* be the reason you refuse Pritchard's offer."

She sucked in several big gulps of air and gave him a death stare. "Go to hell!" she said, and then turned on her heels and left the room.

Interfering, no good, arrogant horse's ass!

Brooke was muttering that and more with every stride as she left the house and trudged toward the stables. Every breath made her madder, every step made her hate Tyler Madden even more.

Hate and love…

Ha! Not a chance, she thought as she grabbed the pitchfork by the door. She could never fall in love with someone who was so filled with self-importance that he couldn't see how very wrong he'd been.

It was unconscionable.

And unforgivable.

Sure…it was a dream offer. But Brooke hadn't even made the decision to sell the small strip of land to Frank Pritchard, let alone just sign the contract and take the money. There was a history of resentment. There was the fact his daughter had been involved in the accident that had killed her parents and sent Matthew running from his guilt and Frank Pritchard's arrogant assurance that nothing would ever be done about it. Now, the very idea that Pritchard would own another small piece of her ranch, especially after the recent rezoning issue, made her sick inside. And angry. And confused. Tyler didn't understand. He was all about winning. About deals. He didn't understand how important it was to stand by her principles, and her family. Hadn't he cruelly sought emancipation from his adoptive parents and never looked back? He obviously lacked heart and the ability to care deeply.

No...that's not true.

She's witnessed firsthand the way he was with Cara. That kind of affection couldn't be feigned. But still, he'd gone too far. As for Werner Stewart, Brooke would be dismissing him as her lawyer as soon as she could. She didn't want deals made behind her back. She didn't want to feel so out of control about her own life. Damn Tyler and his interfering ways.

Jerk.

She hated him.

No, I don't.

Her cell pealed, indicating a text message. She swiped the screen and stared at the text. It was from Matt.

Love you, sis. Merry Christmas.

Gah! Was every man in her life out to make her crazy?

It was Christmas Eve, normally a time when she would be with her friends or at her cousin's ranch, wrapping gifts for Grady's kids or hanging out with Brant or her aunt. But Grady was newly married and it was the first holiday he would be sharing with his bride and three daughters as a family. And with Brant just engaged to her friend Lucy, Brooke didn't want to encroach on their happiness. She'd see them all tomorrow on Christmas Day, as planned. Anyway, she had Cara to think of.

And Tyler.

Brooke did her best to shake off the irritation settled on her shoulders. She didn't want Cara picking up on any tension between them. She stayed outside for a while longer, checking on the hens and the horses. The dogs were playing chase with a stick and she joined in for a few minutes before she locked up the stables and headed back to the house. More snow was forecast overnight and since the evening chores were done a little earlier than usual, she had the luxury of time to hang out with her niece and savor every moment.

Because in two days he would be taking Cara away.

It was clear that Matthew wasn't going to return and, as she trudged back to the house, Brooke decided that if he hadn't called by the following evening, she would have to go against her better judgment and tell him exactly why he needed to come home. She'd tell him about Cara and let the chips fall where they may.

She headed for the shower and once she'd dried off, she slipped into a pale blue knee-length cotton dress that had tiny little white flowers printed on it and teamed it with a soft white sweater, found some comfy shoes, brushed her hair and applied a little lip gloss and left the room. When she reached the living room, she spotted Cara scrambling around on the floor, tossing stuffed toys and grabbing the edge of the sofa. Tyler sat on the edge of the love seat in front of the window, watching the baby. He looked up when he realized she was standing in the doorway and their gazes clashed, and as always, feelings churned through her system, making her more confused, and more vulnerable than ever.

"Hey," he said and placed the laptop on the side table. "Are you okay?"

She nodded a little. "I'm still mad at you."

"I figured."

"But I don't want to waste any of the time I have left with Cara being angry. And I've decided I'm going to tell Matt about her when he calls."

"Okay," he said quietly.

"And if my brother does come back, you did prom-ise you would stay longer so he can get to know her?"

Tyler shrugged one shoulder. "I know what I said. We'll see what happens."

"Fair enough." She moved into the room and managed a tight smile. "Truce?"

"Sure, truce. Friends even."

Shame licked at her heels. "I shouldn't have said we weren't friends. I didn't mean it."

He smiled and was about to get to his feet when both their attentions zeroed in on Cara. Because she was walk-ing, arms outstretched, taking her first, real, wobbly steps by the sofa as she chanted "Dada" over and over and made her way toward Tyler.

Brooke's heart caught behind her ribs and she quickly pulled out her cell phone and began filming the moment, her breath caught on every step, every wobble and every laugh until finally the baby reached the man sitting by the window. Tyler scooped Cara into his arms the instant she connected with his knee and hauled her against his chest.

"Did you see that?" Brooke said with a tiny squeal as she came around the sofa, knowing that of course he had, but unable to contain her excitement.

"I certainly did," he said and stood. "That was quite the expedition for her first time," he laughed with a gri-mace as Cara tugged on a handful of his hair. "I think our girl has been holding out on us."

Our girl...

His words made her heart ache. Because, more than anything else, Brooke wished they were true. She wished Cara was *their* child. And she wished they could watch her grow and nurture her and be a family together—the baby she'd grown to love, and the man who had cap-tured her heart.

She wasn't sure how it had all happened so quickly. Brooke wasn't an impulsive person. She lived a quiet, solitary life, had a few friends and never did anything rash. If anything, she was overcautious, taking her time to get to know people before she let them in. But inside of a week she'd fallen head over heels for the two other people in the room, and was devastated knowing they would probably be ripped from her life in a mere forty-eight hours.

"Brooke?"

She blinked away the emotion burning her eyes. Tyler stood only a few feet from her, watching her, his gaze blazing into her. "We should trim the tree," she suggested and smiled.

He nodded slowly, still watching her. "Sure," he said and passed Cara to her, as if knowing it was exactly what she needed in that moment.

The next few hours flew by in a blur. They trimmed the tree while Christmas music played softly in the background, ate a makeshift dinner of ham and cheese sandwiches, drank coffee, watched Cara play and wobble as she walked some more, and she talked with Tyler about everything from sports to their first high school crushes. Later, they stayed out on the porch and watched the snow begin to fall. Once Cara was fed and tucked up in bed, Tyler stayed with the baby for a few minutes while Brooke wrapped a few birthday presents on the coffee table in the living room.

When he returned, she detoured to the kitchen to wipe down the counters, happy but desperate to not let him see how much the afternoon had meant to her. She certainly didn't want to be caught out making puppy-dog eyes at him. All she had to do was get through the next couple of days...then she could wallow in her broken heart once he was gone.

She checked on Cara and saw her niece was sleeping peacefully, then headed back to the living room. Tyler was on the couch, reading a book. In jeans, a dark green sweater and loafers and dark-rimmed glasses perched on the bridge of his nose, he looked so sexy her mouth turned dry.

"I didn't know you wore reading glasses?"

He looked up and grinned, and her belly did a loop like she was riding a roller coaster way too fast. He removed the glasses and placed them on the coffee table along with the book.

"Do I seem less than perfect to you now?" he teased, his green eyes seeming darker than usual.

Brooke came around the sofa and sat down on the other side. "Perfect? That's a stretch."

He chuckled and the sound hit her way down low. "You look pretty tonight," he said softly. "Actually, you always look beautiful, but tonight, especially so."

Heat smacked her cheeks and she gave a brittle laugh. "You really do need glasses."

His eyes narrowed. "Has some man somewhere along the way told you that you weren't beautiful and you believed him?"

Brooke shrugged, embarrassed that he could read her so easily. "Doyle said that—"

"Doyle's gone," Tyler said, cutting her off and saying her ex-fiancé's name as though it left a sour taste in his mouth. "And he was obviously a faithless fool who didn't appreciate you."

Brooke almost fell into Tyler's arms. How many times had she thought that but had never been able to voice it, too afraid of sounding like a jilted woman scorned?

Doyle *had* told her she wasn't beautiful. Her personality, he'd said, made up for her lack of beauty. Not maliciously, she was certain, but he'd said it often enough to make her believe it.

"Thank you," she said tremulously, almost holding her breath. "It's very sweet of you to say so."

His eyes glittered brilliantly. "Sweet? I don't think I've ever been called that before."

"When you're not being a complete jerk, of course."

He chuckled and then regarded her more soberly. "You know, about today, I didn't mean to overstep the boundaries of our..." He paused, clearly thinking about how to define them, then sighed. "What I'm trying to say is that I'm sorry. As for Pritchard's offer—do what feels right for you, pride and principles included."

Emotion lodged in her throat. He got her. Understood her. Maybe more than anyone ever had before. "I will," she promised. "And...thanks. I probably overreacted a little this afternoon, but I guess I'm not used to having someone go to bat for me." Admitting how alone she was made her insides ache. But there wasn't pity in Tyler's eyes, only understanding. Perhaps because he was alone, too, and knew how it felt. "I heard from Matthew," she said quietly and settled back into the sofa. "He sent a text wishing me a merry Christmas."

"With no mention of returning?"

Brooke shook her head. "Like I said, I think it's time I actually told him about Cara. It might force him to come back."

"It might," he replied. "Or it might make him stay away permanently."

She dropped her shoulders resignedly. "Honestly, I'm not sure what to do. I love my brother, and want him to come home so he can meet his child, but I'm not sure if that's the best thing for Cara anymore. Anyway, before you leave on Saturday I'll give you his number and the last address I had, which was somewhere in New Mexico. I'm certain he's not there now, but you can have it, just the same."

"I'm sorry it's turned out this way, Brooke. I know you'd hoped he would contact you."

She sighed. "Have you booked your flight home?"

"Yes."

"And do you think you could let me know about Cara…about her being adopted? I'd like to be considered," she added softly. "If that's possible."

He reached out and grabbed her hand. "I know you want to care for her, Brooke. And I know it would be what's best for Cara. This past week you've developed a strong bond with her and I can see that it's genuine."

Her heart skipped a beat and she looked to where their hands linked. "Are you saying…are you saying you would consider leaving her here with me?"

He met her gaze levelly. "I can't do that."

Tears burned the back of her eyes. "Oh, I thought—"

"I'm Cara's legal guardian," he said and squeezed her hand gently. "I have a legal and ethical responsibility to follow due process, which means I have to take her back to New York. I'll talk to Ralph, and if he agrees, I'll support your application if you wish to seek custody."

She wanted to weep because it was as though he'd given her the moon. "Thank you."

"I think you'll make a really good mom."

She almost blurted out that he would make a good dad, but she held her tongue. The moment was about Cara, not the silly fantasies Brooke had about the man holding her hand so tenderly. But there was such blistering awareness between them. A connection that defied the short amount of time they'd known one another. Time didn't matter. It was feeling. It was chemistry. It was alchemy and attraction and a deep rooted respect. And she wanted more of it. All of it. All of him. Even if it was only for one moment. Or one precious night.

Brooke met his gaze. "It's been a nice afternoon. Trimming the tree, seeing Cara take her first steps... I'll treasure the memory of it."

"Me, too."

She garnered her courage and stroked the inside of his palm and he tensed instantly. "Tyler... I..."

He dropped her hand and shifted. "We should turn in," he said and got to his feet.

Brooke remained where she was, looking up at him. "Yes," she whispered. "I think we should."

He nodded and stepped away, grabbing his book and glasses. "Well, good night."

She said his name, watched him pause midstride and then met his gaze head-on as she curved her mouth in a soft smile. "I think we should go to bed," she said as she rose to her feet. "Together."

Chapter Ten

Tyler swallowed hard as the meaning of her words sunk into his brain. He stared at her, into her, through her. Her eyes were dark and slumberous. He was drawn into them, mesmerized and stirred at the same time. The room seemed smaller and suddenly Brooke was closer, close enough to touch, close enough to take in his arms.

Good sense should have sent him to his room to take a cold shower. But in that moment, he was all out of good sense. He remained where he was and waited for her to move, to walk from the room and away from temptation. But she didn't. She spoke again, saying his name in that way only she could.

"Tyler…unless my brother returns, you're leaving in two days," she said, reaching out to lay a hand on his chest, where his heart thundered. "Let's not waste the time wondering if this is a good idea or not. We're both cautious. We're both sensible. Maybe…maybe this is about throwing caution to the wind…just for a couple of crazy days."

Uncomplicated, hassle-free, no-pressure sex. A week ago it was all he craved. Now...it seemed as complicated as it could get. Because Brooke wasn't the kind of woman he could love for a night and then leave.

To love...

Damn. He couldn't. He didn't. Did he?

That would be plain old stupid. He was a lot of things, but he'd never considered himself to be a stupid man. He'd always thought romantic love was nonsense, anyway. Friendship and desire were what he believed to be the foundation of a successful relationship. But, somehow... he'd changed since they'd met. She made him think, she made him wonder about his future, about what was important. Being at the ranch, walking the streets of Cedar River, spending time with her and Cara, meeting her family, and even visiting her useless attorney had made him realize how empty his life in New York had become. Within six months he knew he'd be made partner...after that, his life would be set. He'd stay in New York, marry a woman who could deal with the seventy-hour weeks he'd certainly work and then he'd have a couple of kids who would be enrolled in the right school even before they were born.

And in the moment, standing in Brooke's living room, he knew that life was nowhere near as appealing as the offer from the woman in front of him.

He placed his hand over hers. "I thought you said you didn't do crazy and impulsive?"

"I don't," she replied. "But I don't want to have regrets, either. I like being with you. I like the way you make me feel about myself. And I want to keep feeling that for as long as I can."

His blood stirred. Dropping his book and glasses onto the sofa, he pulled her closer, felt her eagerness as she pressed against him. Tyler kissed her, gently fisting a handful of her beautiful hair as he slanted his mouth over hers possessively. When he lifted his head she was breathing hard, her lips full and pink and utterly irresistible.

"We should take the baby monitor with us," she said and pulled back a little.

Tyler nodded and released her, smiling to himself at her practical thinking. He'd meant what he said to her earlier—she'd make a good mother to Cara, and if Ralph agreed, he'd help her gain custody. The ranch would be back on its feet after she signed Pritchard's offer and Cara would be loved and cared for. It was a win-win. Strangely, he still felt hollow inside thinking about it and couldn't figure why.

"Give me a few minutes, okay." He picked up the baby monitor and followed her down the hall, watching as she disappeared into her room. Striding back to his own room, he grabbed the birth control tucked into his suitcase pocket and then headed to her room. She was by the bed, sweater and shoes gone, simply standing there in her pretty dress, hair flowing over her shoulders, her skin dappled in the lamplight. Her bedroom was what he'd expected, neat and tidy with a few pieces of furniture and a sensible blue quilt on the bed.

He placed the baby monitor and the foil packet on the bedside table and met her gaze. "Okay?"

She glanced at the contraception and nodded. "Yes… only, you don't really need that."

"I know you don't sleep around, Brooke," he assured her. "Neither do I. But I also don't play roulette with birth control."

Her gaze narrowed. "I understand."

She seemed tense and he remained where he was. "If you're having second thoughts about this, that's okay."

"I'm not," she whispered. "I want you to make love to me, Tyler. It's all I want."

He took three steps and reached for her, holding her close, drawing her against him as he ran his hands down her back and hips. She wound her arms around him, clutching at his back, and then met his lips without hesitation as he kissed her deeply.

They made it to the bed, still wrapped in one another's arms. He laid her down, kissing her jaw, her throat, the delicate skin near her collarbone. The buttons on her dress came undone easily and he flicked them open as he kissed her. Her tongue met his, dancing and sliding as he pushed the dress off her shoulders. She wore a white lace bra, modest by current trends, but incredibly sexy against her smooth skin. Her nipples pressed hard against the fabric and he groaned low in his throat, teasing the buds through the lace with his thumb. She arched her back, exposing her neck, begging for his mouth against her body. Her skin tasted so good and he craved her more with each kiss, each touch and each stroke.

Her hands were on his back, his shoulders, his chest, hot and demanding through the clothing he wore. She lay on the mattress, wearing only her white lace underwear, and he took a second to admire her curves, from the swell of her generous breasts to her curvy hips and thighs. Womanly, he thought as desire spiked through him, sending all the blood rushing to his groin. She looked exactly how he'd imagined. Exactly what he craved.

"You're staring at me," she said self-consciously, flushing.

"Because you're beautiful," he said raggedly and

traced his knuckles between her breasts and then over her belly. "And I'm just about lost for words right now."

She smiled as her eyes darkened. "Then stop talking and make love to me."

Tyler chuckled softly. He liked that about her, that she wasn't serious and tried to ease the tension. He kissed her again as he pushed the bra strap off one shoulder and then the other. He reached around and flicked the clasp, freeing her breasts to fall into his hands. When he closed his mouth over one hardened nipple he thought he might pass out. She moaned as he caressed her with his tongue, grasping his neck and urging him closer, and Tyler had never been more turned on in his life. He pushed her briefs over her hips in one smooth movement and once she was naked his gaze traveled up and down, lingering over every sexy inch of her.

"You're staring again," she whispered, pushing her fingers through his hair.

"I can't help it," he admitted in a raspy voice. "Your body is—"

"Too curvy," she said, cutting him off.

He shook his head. "Perfect. Sexy. Gorgeous."

She smiled. "Well, I'm glad you think so. Speaking of all things perfectly sexy," she said and tugged playfully at his collar, "you're wearing way too many clothes right now."

His shoes, shirt, jeans and briefs were off in about three seconds flat. Naked, they fit together perfectly. Then they kissed some more, hot, deep kisses that almost drove him off the edge. But he held back, wanting to love her right, wanting to somehow imprint his skin and soul on her, so she'd never forget their time together. Like he knew he'd never forget.

Tyler smoothed his hand over her hips as she arched

forward, welcoming his intimate touch. She moaned as he created a steady rhythm, her face flushed, her lips parted slightly as she was drawn deeper into pleasure. Her seductive groan was all the encouragement he needed to take her to the edge and back, and finally when he knew she could stand no more, he gave her the release she craved. As he watched her and saw her beautiful face flush as pleasure pulsed through her, Tyler felt as though two hands had reached inside his chest and squeezed his heart.

He grabbed the condom and she took it from him with a lovely smile. Within seconds he was ready and over her, resting on his elbows. She said his name, meeting his gaze. Her eyes were bright, shining, her emotions on display. He swallowed the lump in his throat and then he kissed her again, capturing her mouth gently, and experienced a strange sensation deep down, as though everything he was feeling was suddenly amplified—his desire for her, the way he liked the sound of her husky voice, the way she made him smile without really trying. That's what drew him to her. He wanted her. He liked her. He needed her. Suddenly it felt as though he needed her like he needed air to breathe. And the realization knocked him sideways. He'd never needed anyone, never laid himself or his heart on the line. No one had ever got to him. Until now.

The exact moment she realized she really was in love with Tyler, Brooke had to fight back the tears. She didn't want to cry in the middle of making love with him, but her nerves, her emotions, every fiber that went soul deep, was heightened by the feelings running riot throughout her body and mind. Love, as bright and incandescent as a star in the heavens, flowed through her. Being with him, feeling him over her and then inside her, was like nothing she'd experienced before. Sure, in the past, making love had often been pleasurable, but it had never felt like this.

"Are you okay?" he asked softly.

Brooke nodded, her belly tied up in knots. "I'm fine. I'm…good. This…feels…good."

He kissed her cheek, his breath warm against her skin as he nibbled on her earlobe. "It most certainly does."

Brooke ran her hands along his back. His muscles flexed beneath her touch and the smattering of hair on his chest created a delightful friction against her flesh. His body was perfectly sculpted, smooth and strong. She clung to him, shameless and aroused and so much in love she could barely contain her happiness. Of course, she knew it wouldn't last. He was leaving soon and taking Cara with him, but for this moment, he was hers, and she could pretend that it was for more than one night.

She pressed her hands into his hips, urging him closer, deeper, needing him like she needed air in her lungs. He moved slowly, watching her with such burning, erotic intensity she was sure she got lost in his gaze. When the pressure built, when they could take it no more, release came to them both and as he shuddered above her, she clung to him, caught up in a vortex of pleasure so intense she could only whisper his name as though it was the only word she knew.

When he eventually rolled off her, Brooke took a few long, steadying breaths, her body still pulsing with tiny aftershocks. He grabbed her hand, kissing her knuckles as he excused himself for a moment. He returned from the bathroom a minute or so later, still naked and aroused, and was about to grab the baby monitor when Brooke pushed back the bedcovers with a smile and invited him to join her between the sheets.

"You're sure?" he asked.

"That I want you to stay the night in my bed?" She moved the covers some more, showing a considerable amount of skin. "Absolutely."

He slipped into the bed without any more encouragement and drew her against him. They kissed and touched for a while and then Tyler gently pushed her hair back from her face and told her how beautiful she was. Brooke touched his jaw, felt the soft bristle of five o'clock shadow.

"You didn't shave today," she mused. "That's not like you."

"No," he said and kissed her temple. "I had other things on my mind."

She sighed and stretched. "I like it. It's sexy."

They kissed again and then slowly the heat subsided, to be replaced by a gentleness that made her sleepy and longing for the chance to close her eyes. And dream.

It was Cara gurgling through the baby monitor that woke Brooke at dawn. She'd managed a few hours' sleep after they'd made love again around midnight. She was alone in bed and ignored the tiny stab of disappointment as she stretched, thinking how lovely the night had been, and then pushed the covers back. The floor was cold on her feet so she stepped into her slippers, grabbed the thick robe at the bottom of the bed and padded out to the hallway and toward Cara's room.

"I tried not to wake you when I got up," Tyler said when he saw her.

"You didn't," she assured him. "I heard you and Cara talking on the monitor."

"Talking?" He grinned and rested the baby on his hip. "Not sure I would call it that."

Brooke came into the room and grasped Cara's hand.

"Looks like *dada* has become her favorite word." Cara started mumbling incoherently and it made them both chuckle.

"She's a birthday girl today," he reminded her.

"Yes, I know."

He met her gaze. "And merry Christmas, Brooke."

"Gosh, I forgot," she said and shrugged. "It is Christmas. So, how about I quickly go and see to the animals and then make breakfast? After that we can watch Cara tear open the presents we got her and then stand back while she plays with the wrapping paper instead of the toys."

He laughed and the sound made her so warm and happy that Brooke couldn't help but move in close and stand on her toes to kiss his cheek. "Looks like it was snowing overnight, but it seems clear now. Maybe later we could go for a walk and build a snowman with Cara? We don't need to be at Grady's until after lunch."

He nodded and curled an arm around her waist. Together, just the three of them, filled Brooke with such a sense of completeness she could barely draw a breath. Cara was chuckling, Tyler was smiling and in that moment Brooke was happier than she'd ever been in her life.

Family...

The word rolled around in her head, making her delirious. Tyler dropped a kiss to her hair and she pressed against him, loving the feel of his hard, strong body against her. And she wanted to take a snapshot of the moment and hold on to it forever.

She took off back to her bedroom and dressed in jeans, sweater and jacket, and pulled her boots on by the back door. She fed the dogs, the chickens, let the horses out of the stables and filled up the hay feeder, and twenty minutes later she was back inside. After she washed up and

changed her shirt she headed for the kitchen and Brooke
made breakfast and put on a pot of coffee.

"Animals all done?"

Tyler's voice caught her attention. He was by the door,
Cara in his arms as the little girl pulled his hair and called
him "Dada." It was such an endearing picture and her
womb rolled over. To share a child with this man would
be a dream come true. All she ever wanted. And she
mourned the notion that it could never be.

"Yes," she said and blinked away the heat in her eyes.
"I thought you could make pancakes."

"Sounds good," he said and grinned. "I'm onto it."

The pancakes were fabulous and she had to admit he
was a much better cook than she was. Once they were done
eating, she scooped Cara from the high chair and walked
to the living room. Tyler was behind her and within minutes Cara was opening both birthday and Christmas gifts.
As expected, the crinkly paper got most of her attention
and they laughed when she crawled over the toys to tear
the wrapping with her tiny fists.

Tyler disappeared for a minute and returned with a
small brown carry bag, which he immediately passed
to her.

"What's this?" she asked, sitting cross-legged on the
floor with the baby as she peered inside the bag.

"Take a look."

She frowned slightly. "You bought me a gift?"

He shrugged. "It's just something I thought you would
like."

"I didn't get you anything."

He shrugged, looking faintly embarrassed. "It's just
a small thing. No big deal."

Brooke took the flat parcel out of the bag and un-
wrapped the tissue paper. It was a framed photograph of

Cara. The baby's smiling face stared out from the print and it made Brooke's insides crunch up. A way to remember Cara once he was gone. Is that why he'd given her the gift? Because he knew he was taking Cara away? He'd said he'd support her custody application, but she knew that could take months. She tried to look grateful, even happy, but her smile faded before it began.

"Everything okay?" he asked, clearly sensing her mood.

She ached in her heart knowing what the gift really meant. Glancing up, she was mesmerized by the look in his green eyes. "Of course. Thank you. It's perfect. When did you get this done?"

"The other day when I was in town."

Brooke's mouth curled. "When you were doing errands?"

He looked sheepish for moment, as though he didn't want to be reminded of his high-handed interference. "Well, I—"

"It's okay," she said softly. "I've forgiven you for the whole Pritchard thing. And I'm going to accept the offer," she said and nodded. "You were right...it was a pride thing. Probably some hangover from when my parents were alive and how Frank was always trying to get his hands on some of the land and my dad was always refusing. But I have a responsibility to this ranch and to its legacy," she said and looked toward Cara. "I want custody of Cara. I want to make her a home here, one where she is safe and secure. And to do that I need to forget about pride and use good sense."

He didn't move. "I'm glad."

"Do you think I have a chance," she said and shrugged one shoulder. "Of getting custody, I mean? In your professional opinion."

"I'll talk to Ralph," he replied, giving little away. "Yelena's wish was always that Cara would be with her father. But Ralph was less than impressed with her relationship with your brother. He knew Matt wasn't going to hang around, despite what had been said to Yelena. But, you're her family, too, and I'll do my best to make him see that Cara belongs here with you."

"Thank you," she said, swallowing hard. "It means a lot to me to hear you say that…considering how we had such a rocky start."

He grinned slightly as his eyes darkened. "Oh, I'd say we were getting along just fine now."

Now. Because they'd had sex. Even though for Brooke it had been much more than that. Making love with Tyler had cemented the indisputable fact that she was in love with him. Wholly and completely. Knowing she would probably be losing him in twenty-four hours felt like a stab in her lovesick heart.

"It was…nice," she said softly.

His brows shot up. "Nice?"

Color quickly burned her cheeks. "You know what I mean."

Tyler smiled and held out his hand. Brooke wound her fingers around his and let him pull her to her feet. He pressed toward her, curving her body to his. "*Nice* kind of makes me think of walks in the park and puppies. Last night was incredible."

Before she could respond he kissed her deeply, each slant of his mouth a seductive caress. Brooke gave herself to him, matching the gentle slide of his tongue. Despite their mutual passion, there was something else in the kiss… It was familiar and sweet and had an intensity that made her knees weak. When he lifted his head she saw him smiling.

"See," he said, his eyes so dark they looked ocean deep. "Incredible."

She laughed, delighted and so in love in that moment nothing could have possibly dampened her spirits. "Let's go for a walk?" she suggested.

He nodded and released her reluctantly. "I'll get Cara's coat and stroller. We'll see how we go wheeling it through the snow."

"Stop whining like a city boy," she teased. "We'll drag it if we have to. It will be fun. I promise."

Ten minutes later they were outside, both wheeling *and* dragging the stroller with a laughing and delighted Cara warmly tucked inside. Brooke had dressed in jeans and her favorite red sweater, and denim jacket with her winter coat over the top. She left her hair loose and had pulled a colored beanie on her head. Time flew by too fast, she thought as they roamed around the house, tossing snowballs at one another at regular intervals, which made Cara laugh even harder.

"I'm going to get you back for that one," Tyler warned playfully as he wiped the remnants of a snowball from his face. "Just so you know."

Brooke laughed happily and tossed some more snow in his direction. "I'm hoping you do."

The mood between them was friendly and familiar with just enough of an undercurrent of awareness to keep her remembering how they'd been making love barely hours earlier. As they walked a little farther past the fence perimeter she couldn't help thinking how it all felt so normal, so *real*. The dogs were barking in the distance, no doubt where she left them on the porch with instructions to stay, but still not happy they'd been left behind. They were about half a mile from the house when the stroller got lodged deep in a drift and they both dropped to their haunches to scoop snow from around the wheels.

"Told you so," Tyler said, grinning.

Brooke regarded him leisurely. In jeans and a white shirt, dark blue sweater, boots and a coat he looked ridiculously handsome and yet, right in his element. He'd fit anywhere, she realized. Penthouse or ranch house. And for a few wistful moments she wished he'd stay exactly where he was, frozen in time, indelibly carved in her memory bank for all eternity.

She shoved him playfully and he did the same and within seconds he was lying over her, while Cara squealed and laughed inches away in her snowbound stroller. He kissed her hot and hard, and she pushed her hands into his frosted hair. He held her head and moaned softly against her mouth, one leg pressed intimately between her thighs. Brooke vaguely thought she heard a sound, but was so wrapped up in Tyler's kisses that all logical thought turned to mush. In that moment he was hers and she was his and nothing could ruin the mood.

Nothing except someone clearing their throat and then a familiar voice speaking.

"Well, this sure isn't what I expected to come back to."

Tyler moved instantly and Brooke blinked a few times and then stared at a pair of jean-clad legs and heavy work boots standing in the snow a few feet away. Her breath caught as her gaze traveled up until she met a familiar pair of eyes so blue they were almost violet.

Her long-lost brother had come home.

Tyler was up and on his heels the moment he realized that Matthew Laughton was glaring down at them as though he'd witnessed a crime scene. Having met the younger man several times when Matt was dating Yelena, he had as little regard for him then as he did now. Maybe more so. Because now Cara and Brooke were swept up in Matt Laughton's wake of disaster…and they were the two people he cared about most in the world.

He ignored the twitch in his gut at the sight of the younger man and quickly grabbed Brooke's hand to help her up. Once she was standing she released his hand and within seconds was in her brother's embrace. He ignored the resentment curdling his blood and stepped beside the stroller protectively.

"Gosh, it's good to see you," Brooke said breathlessly and hugged her brother again.

Matthew held her away from him and smiled. "And you." His gaze flicked to the stroller and then Tyler. "Ah…what's going on here? Who is—" He stopped mid-sentence as recognition hit. "Hey, I know you…you're—"

"Tyler Madden. Ralph Jürgens's lawyer," Tyler supplied coolly.

Matthew Laughton's eyes darkened. "Yelena," he said so quietly it was almost to the wind. "Yelena," he said her name again. "Is she here?"

"No," Tyler said, biting back the urge to throw a punch. He wasn't violent, but Matthew's arrival had somehow put him off his guard.

The other man frowned. "I don't understand what's going on here?" He glanced at his sister, then back to Tyler, scowling harder. "And what the hell was that I just saw between you and my—"

"That," Brooke said swiftly and grasped her brother's arm, "is definitely none of your business. But there is something you need to know. I didn't want to tell you in a text so—"

"Tell me what?" he demanded, cutting off his sister's words. He looked toward Tyler and then the stroller. "And why is there a baby here? What the hell is going on?" He looked at Brooke, still scowling. "Why have you been sending me urgent texts all week and why the hell were you rolling around in the snow with this guy when—"

"Enough!" Tyler said the word so harshly that he saw Brooke wince. But it shut Matthew Laughton up immediately. He took a deep breath and spoke again. "First, don't ever talk to your sister that way. And second, this is Cara," he said, gesturing to the baby happily gurgling in the stroller. "She's Yelena Jürgens's child," he said the words slowly, so that Matthew would understand every word. "And your daughter."

The younger man stepped back and flicked off his sister's hand. His gaze moved to the baby suspiciously. "My daughter?" he said the words incredulously. "I don't believe it."

Brooke stepped closer. "It's true, Matt. Cara is your child."

"It's not possible," he said, shaking his head. "We always used protection and—"

"Birth control can fail," Tyler said and tried to diffuse the anger he experienced, sensing Matt didn't want to immediately embrace the idea that Cara was his. Couldn't he see how precious she was?

If she were mine I would claim her in a heartbeat. And Brooke.

"She's your child," Tyler said coolly. "But I can arrange DNA testing if you need it."

"Matt." Brooke's voice rang out gently. "It's true. I've seen the birth certificate. Look at her," she implored with such feeling it made Tyler's insides ache. "She's a Laughton. She's such a beautiful child and once you get to know her you'll fall in love with her, too."

Matthew shook his head, clearly shocked and outraged. "No," he said and stepped back. "It's impossible. No way in hell," he said as he turned and walked off.

Tyler waited until he was twenty feet in the distance before he turned back toward Brooke. She had tears in her eyes. He wanted to take her in his arms, but he was so angry with her brother he knew it wasn't the time.

"I'll talk to him," she offered.

Tyler pulled the stroller out of the snow and pushed it forward. "Do that, and soon," he said coldly. "Because time is running out."

Chapter Eleven

By the time they reached the house Brooke's emotions were hanging by a thread. Matt was home. It was Christmas Day. And Cara's birthday. They should be getting ready to celebrate the day with her aunt and cousins at Grady's ranch. Instead she was entering the house with knots in her stomach. The fact that Tyler walked beside her, his expression carved from stone, didn't help appease the uncertainty of her thoughts.

I need to fix this.

She summoned her strength and walked into the house. Tyler didn't follow her from the kitchen and she suspected he was heading to put Cara down for a nap. Brooke walked into the living room and spotted her brother by the window. He'd grown up, she thought as she watched him. Five years had turned him from a boy into a man. He was nearly twenty-four. He'd been alone, living his life, making his way in the world.

And making a baby.

"Matt," she said as she moved around the sofa. "We really need to talk about this."

He stood rigid, his back to her. When he finally turned she saw the emotion in his eyes. He was clearly hanging on by a thread. "Are you sure? Is it really true?"

"That she's your daughter? Yes," Brooke assured him. "It's true. She looks just like you, Matt. And why would Yelena lie about such a thing? You did have an intimate relationship with her, right?"

He nodded. "Yes. And the lawyer…what's he got to do with this?"

"Tyler brought Cara here. It was Yelena's wish."

Matt closed his eyes for a second, blinking hard. "Where is Yelena? Something's happened, hasn't it?" he asked and didn't wait for a reply. "I mean, to Yelena. It must have, otherwise she'd be here telling me all this."

"She passed away a few months ago," Brooke said as she nodded and then calmly explained what she knew about Yelena's illness and pregnancy. "That's all I know. If you need more information you need to talk to Tyler."

"Tyler?" he quizzed. "You two looked very friendly out there in the snow."

She ignored the heat spotting her cheeks. "That's not up for discussion. All that matters is Cara."

"Cara," he echoed softly and sat down as though the world weighed down on his shoulders "It's a pretty name. Yelena always liked that name."

"You talked about baby names?" Brooke asked quickly.

He shrugged wearily. "It was just talk. I think it was her mom's name or something. Damn," he said and ran a hand through his floppy blond hair. "Why didn't she tell me she was pregnant?"

"Because she didn't have your number after you ran out."

Tyler's voice, cool and calm from the doorway, turned Brooke's head instantly. Her first instinct was to run to her brother's defense. But she was torn, conflicted, desperate to remain a unified front with the man she loved, but unwilling to hurt her little brother.

Matt was scowling. "Yelena knew I wasn't hanging around," he said defensively. "Look, I liked her, okay. I liked her a lot. But she knew I had a job offer in Seattle and I was up front about it from the start. I've been working in construction, remodeling old homes. It's turned into something," he said and looked toward Brooke, searching her face for support. "I've got my own crew and I'm doing well, making money, and I bought a house six months ago."

"I'm happy for you, Matt," she said softly. "I'm happy that you've made a life for yourself. But we need to talk about Cara's future."

He rubbed a hand down his face. "It's a lot to get my head around."

"Of course," she said gently. "But she's a baby and she needs her father. It's what Yelena wanted."

He looked up and met her gaze, then shot a look toward Tyler. "Is that true?"

Tyler's expression was hard, without feeling. And she realized that in that moment he was all lawyer, all process and procedure. "Yes. She wanted Cara to be with her father."

Matt got to his feet and paced the room. "I don't know," he said, sounding hopeless. "This is a big shock. I came back expecting you to tell me you'd sold the place or you were getting married or something," he said and flicked his gaze between her and Tyler. "I wasn't expecting to learn I'm a father. So," he said, a little firmer as he looked toward Tyler again, "where do you fit into this scenario?"

"Ralph Jürgens appointed me as Cara's legal guardian."

Matt nodded slowly. "So, basically, that means you're calling all the shots?"

"Exactly."

Brooke couldn't stand how quickly the tension was escalating between the two men. She knew Tyler wouldn't give an inch. His job was to protect Cara and he would do that to his last breath. She also knew her brother... and that's what terrified her.

"You have to come home, Matt," she said firmly. "You have to come home and be a father. You have a responsibility to that little girl. She needs you."

He sighed heavily. "Like I said, I need time to get my head around this."

"You have until tomorrow to decide," Brooke pointed out, harsher than she liked, but she was desperate for her brother to do what was right.

"Tomorrow?" he echoed and then looked at Tyler. "Are you kidding? Is that your doing?"

Brooke watched, fascinated, as Tyler stood as still as a statue, his expression impassive, giving nothing away. But she knew he wasn't as unaffected as he wanted to make out. The tiny pulse in his cheek throbbed and his broad shoulders were tighter than she'd ever seen them. She knew his moods, she'd witnessed them over the past week as she was falling in love with him. He knew her, too, she was sure. He knew she was devastated at the thought of losing Cara.

"I agreed to stay a week," Tyler said so formally she

actually shivered. "Your sister assured me you would return."

"Well, she was right," Matt said and smiled a little. "I'm here. But I need more than twenty-four hours to work out what I'm going to do. Look," he said, hands on hips. "I get that there's an innocent child involved here, but I just found out I have a daughter less than an hour ago, so how about you give me a break and get off my back."

Brooke stilled, refusing to take a breath in case she missed a word of Tyler's response. Part of her admired her brother for standing up for himself. He *had* grown up. She only hoped he'd grown up enough. Glancing at Tyler, she could see that he was angry, but she knew he'd control himself—because he was always in control.

"I promised your sister that I would give you some time with Cara if you came back. So, I'll stay until Wednesday," he said evenly. "That's when I'll make my decision."

"Your decision?" Matt asked, scowling.

"Yelena wanted her daughter to be with her father. *If*, and only if, I think you are what's best for Cara, then I will agree to you taking over custody. But don't press your luck with me, Laughton. All I care about is what happens to that little girl down the hall."

Brooke got to her feet, suddenly afraid the two men might come to blows. Matt had always been a hothead and she sensed that although Tyler appeared to have a long fuse, he might be the same if pushed too hard.

"How about I make coffee," she suggested.

Matt shook his head, still staring at Tyler. "I'd like to go and meet my daughter…if that's okay with you."

Tyler nodded slowly and placed the baby monitor on

the sideboard. "Sure, second room on the right," he said quietly, making it very clear he would be listening.

For a second she thought Matt was going to get riled up, but instead he shrugged loosely and cast Brooke a weary look before he slowly left the room.

She waited until his footsteps faded before she spoke. "Was that necessary?"

Tyler met her gaze. "What?"

"Making him feel about a foot tall."

He dropped a shoulder. "He needs to know how things stand. Pandering to him isn't going to help the situation."

"Pandering?" Brooke echoed as irritation crept over her skin.

Tyler's expression remain granite hard. "He's a grown man and needs to act like one."

"We need to give him a chance." She shot back. "Naturally, he's in shock."

"Naturally."

The baby monitor crackled and Matt's voice came through, soft and low as he talked to the baby, who was clearly awake and gurgling. "See," she said and half smiled. "He's doing okay. He's here and he's trying."

"We'll see."

She stayed calm, even though her temper flared inside. He was being as unyielding as a rock. "I really want this to work out," she said. "I understand you have a job to do, but please, don't make it harder for my brother than it already is."

"I'll do my best."

She knew he was annoyed, could feel it in his cool tone. "And thank you for agreeing to stay a little longer... I know you have a life that you have to get back to. I know you—"

"Do you?" he snapped and ran a hand through his

hair. "Do you really? Do you know how conflicted I am at the moment?"

"Of course," she said, stepping closer. "You're attached to Cara and—"

"This isn't about Cara," he flipped back, his green eyes boring into her. "It's about you."

He was conflicted about her? "Me?"

"You," he said again. "Us."

Us...

Brooke almost swooned. "But I didn't think—"

"You didn't think what?" he demanded and reached for her, pulling her against him. "That it wouldn't be hard for me to leave you? No?" he queried, his eyes scorching hers. "Do you think I'm made of stone?"

The ragged passion in his voice rendered her mindless and she sagged against him. His strong arms moved around her, and he held her with a kind of fierce possession she hadn't experienced before. He gently fisted a handful of her hair, tilted her head back and kissed her hotly, like he was suddenly quenching an insatiable thirst. Brooke kissed him back and they stayed like that until Matt's voice pulled them back into reality.

"Ah...so, I think she needs a diaper change or something."

He released her abruptly and Brooke stepped away, conscious that her brother had caught her making out with Tyler twice in as many hours.

"I'll take care of it," Tyler said, not looking at her as he turned and strode from the room.

Once he was gone, Matt let out a low whistle. "Speaking of all things unexpected... I didn't think I'd come home to catch you in a lip-lock with Ice Man."

Brooke frowned. "Don't, Matt. He's not like that."

Her brother's eyes widened. "Oh, Jesus, don't tell me you've actually fallen for him?"

Completely and totally.

"I don't want to talk about it. Tell me where you've been," she said, flipping the subject. "Seattle, you said?"

He shrugged lightly. "Yeah, for the past twenty months or so. I love what I'm doing and there's plenty of restoration work happening. When I first left here I headed for New Mexico and worked my way on a few construction sites. I met an old guy, an old-time builder who kind of took me under his wing. He taught me what he knew. When he died a couple of years ago his ashes were flown back to Boston, where he was from. From there I went to New York," he explained. "And then I met Yelena." He paused, thinking, clearly remembering. "It's a damned awful thing, her dying."

"Yes, it is."

Matt's eyes softened. "But the baby, she's really beautiful."

Brooke's heart swelled up. "I'm so glad you feel that way. Do you...do you want her, Matt?"

"How could I not?" he replied. "I mean, she's my kid. Of course...of course I want her. I think I just need some time to adjust to all this. It kind of came out of the blue."

"I didn't want to tell you in a text message," she said. "I hope you understand that."

He shrugged. "I do. And it's really good to see you. I've missed you." He looked around the room. "And I've missed this place. Although it's a bit run-down since the last time I was here."

She shrugged loosely. "I know. I haven't done a great job of maintaining things. But it's been hard doing it..."

"Alone?" he said when her words trailed off. "Yeah, I guess that's on me. I left you to handle it all."

Brooke's chest tightened. "I don't blame you, Matt. I think I did at first…but not anymore. You're my little brother and I love you. And I've missed you."

"I've missed you, too," he admitted, his voice thick with emotion. "I've missed this place. I used to think I'd always live on this ranch and be a part of this town. But everything changed that day…you know…after the accident."

Heat burned her eyes. "It was a long time ago. Have you made peace, Matt? Have you made peace with yourself?"

He looked into her eyes. "Honestly, I don't know," he said and sighed. "I've tried to make a good life in Seattle… one that's got some value, even though I can never make up for what happened. I've tried to be the kind of man that our parents would be proud of. Even though I still screw up sometimes," he said and managed a wry smile. "Like I did with Yelena."

"Did you love her, Matt?"

He shrugged. "She was a nice girl. Sweet…a little lost, I guess…like me. We just kind of drifted together and then we drifted apart."

Brooke's brows came up. "You drifted apart?"

He immediately looked sheepish. "Okay… I bailed. She knew I wasn't staying in New York permanently, but once she started getting serious I guess I spooked and left. Yeah," he said when Brooke shook her head. "I know… I'm a jerk." He took a deep breath. "But I want to make things right by Yelena. And by my daughter."

Brooke gave him a hug. "I'm so pleased to hear you say that. You're home now, and that's all that matters."

"Yeah," he said soberly. "I guess I am."

But the vagueness in his voice couldn't be missed.

* * *

The Parker Ranch was a big, sprawling spread, like the type seen on postcards or vacation posters in travel agency windows. And Tyler couldn't help thinking how much Brooke would love a place just like it. How she *deserved* a place just like it. Since she'd decided to take Pritchard's offer he was hopeful she'd be able to restore the ranch to what he figured it once was. He'd be long gone by then. Back in New York and ensconced in his old life.

Yet every time he looked at her, he was drawn further in, deeper, making the idea of leaving her harder. But now that Matthew had returned and said he was prepared to be a father to Cara, Tyler could actually see an end in sight. Of course, he had reservations. His opinion of Matt hadn't changed in a matter of hours. But Yelena had been convinced that Matthew would be up to the task of being a parent and Tyler knew he needed to be open to the idea out of respect for her dying wishes. Ultimately, he would do what was best for Cara. Either way, for him, there would be no Brooke. No Cara. Just the life he'd been entrenched in for so many years he'd forgotten there was something else possible, something more.

First thing he needed to do was rearrange his flights and contact the office to tell them of his changed schedule. He was pretty sure the senior partner wouldn't be happy he was stretching the trip out a few more days, but it couldn't be helped. Cara's future was more important to him than…

Than anything.

The realization had slowly worked its way into his head that morning. That he loved the baby. She had wheedled her way into his heart. She'd made him a better man. Being with Cara and Brooke had filled an emptiness he hadn't had the courage to acknowledge. But he could now.

He loved Brooke.

He'd never been in love before, had always avoided too much commitment, figuring he had time before he settled down. But hell, who was he kidding? At thirty-four years old he'd fallen in love for the first time. And he was in love with a woman who lived thousands of miles from him. A cowgirl. A woman who loved her ranch and her horses as though they were the blood that flowed through her veins. She could never do the city...and after nearly twenty years it was all he knew.

There was no middle road for them.

"Everything okay with you?"

He turned and discovered that Colleen Parker had sidled up beside him. He was on the front porch, braving the cold air after spending over an hour being suffocated by all the familial closeness. The Parkers were a happy and somewhat noisy family who obviously cared about one another a great deal. If Matt could prove he could be a responsible parent, Cara would be well loved, he was sure of it. Still, the ache that had steadily developed all day now felt like a hole he might never be able to fill.

"Yes, of course."

The older woman's eyes were wide and curious. "So, how do you think young Matt is going to do as a full-time dad?"

"Time will tell."

"Yes," Colleen said. "I can see you have your reservations as I do. I'm not sure he's grown up enough yet for the job."

"He's her father. In the eyes of the law, that's usually what matters most."

"I've always believed that when it comes to family,"

she said with a wise smile, "that it's the heart that matters most."

He shrugged loosely. "Maybe. But it's also what Yelena wanted."

"She was young," Colleen said. "And probably too in love with that young man inside to see him clearly. Oh, don't get me wrong, Matthew is a kind and caring person and I'm sure he'll do the best he can...but Cara needs more than good intentions."

"He'll have his sister to help him through the hard times."

"Yes," Colleen said, her eyes wide. "Brooke always has been a tower of strength. And she's one of the kindest, most loyal people I have ever known. But I think you already know that." She tapped his arm affectionately and then waved an arm in an arc. "I know you have a life far away from here...but don't be too quick to leave all this behind."

"Different worlds," he said cryptically and crossed his arms.

"Yes. And sometimes worlds collide." Her expression softened. "My niece has had a lot of hurt and disappointment in her life...perhaps more than you know. I do hope you're not going to be another page in that book."

She smiled and walked back inside. He could hear the family laughing and talking through the open door and he almost envied them. With that thought he pulled out his cell phone and flicked through the numbers on speed dial. He selected a number and waited for the call to connect.

"Hello."

Recognition warmed his chest. "Hey, Mom."

"Tyler." His mother breathed his name in her wispy voice. "It's so good to hear your voice."

Four months, he thought guiltily. It had been that long

since he'd bothered to contact his parents. "You, too. How's Dad?"

She chuckled. "Good. He's in the kitchen carving the roast."

Tyler smiled to himself. His parents were longtime vegans, so he figured their roast was some kind of soy or tofu offering. "Glad to hear you're keeping him busy." He paused, fighting the emotion suddenly in his throat. "Ah...merry Christmas, Mom."

"Merry Christmas, son."

His mother sniffed and he suspected she was already crying. "So," he said, trying to lighten the mood, and the reception crackled. "I was thinking of coming for a visit."

She was silent for a second. "A visit? Really? That would be wonderful. When?"

"Soon," he promised.

They chatted for a couple of minutes and when he finally said goodbye he couldn't believe how much better he felt. He turned to go back inside, but found Brooke standing by the door, one shoulder leaning against the jamb.

"I wasn't eavesdropping," she said and smiled as she pushed herself off the door frame and moved toward him. "I just didn't want to interrupt you. You were talking to your parents?"

"Yes, to my mother."

"I'm glad. It's important to connect with family at this time of year."

He knew he had her to thank for it and nodded fractionally. "So, how's the new dad doing in there?" he asked, eager to talk about anything other than himself.

"Pretty good," she replied and laughed. "Matt changed his first diaper. Under Colleen's strict supervision, of course, and he seemed to catch on quickly. Although he did look a little green around the gills."

Tyler laughed and damn it felt good. The last few hours had been unbearably strained. "I'm sure he'll get used to it."

She stepped in beside him, so close he picked up traces of the scent that was uniquely hers. He was about to move when she grabbed his hand and linked their fingers. He looked down and saw her eyes glittering.

"What is it?"

"Thank you," she whispered. "Thank you for carrying out Yelena's wishes and giving Matt this chance."

"It's my job."

She squeezed his hand. "I know it's more than that. Ralph is your friend and I know you're genuinely attached to Cara. But it's more than that. You're a good person...kind and considerate."

"I thought I was an arrogant jerk?" he chided softly, reminding her of her name-calling.

"A lot can change in a week," she said and released his hand. "But now Matt is home, I think everything will be okay."

"I hope you're right."

"Are you coming back inside?" she asked. "It's Christmas, so don't be alone out here."

"I'm not alone," he said and grabbed her hand again, and then they walked back inside. Together.

When they got home that evening it was close to nine o'clock. Tyler hung back while Matt put his daughter to bed, and then Matt said he was beat and excused himself to go to his room. But Cara seemed restless so Tyler sat in the chair by her crib a little while, winding the nursey rhyme mobile over and over until she drifted off.

"She's had a big day," Brooke said, meeting him in

the doorway. "And I think she's probably used to your voice singing her to sleep."

His insides crunched up. "Maybe."

"So... I was wondering," she said, looking up, all indigo eyes and pink lips. "Are you going to your room, or mine?"

His libido did a mad leap. All he wanted to do was carry her down the hall, strip off her clothes and make love to her all night long. But things were different tonight. "Do you think that's wise since your brother is here?"

She tugged on her lower lip with her teeth and reached up, her palm on his chest. "He's my brother, not my father. And since he's caught us making out twice already today, I think he's got a fair idea about what's going on."

God, she was messing with his head. "I don't think we should complicate things any further, do you?"

She looked hurt. "You don't want me?"

"It's not that," he said, dying inside. "I just need to stay focused on what's important."

Her hand dropped. "Oh... I see. Okay, good night, then."

"Good night." The words clawed their way off his tongue because the last thing he wanted to do was leave her bed for the solitary coldness of his own.

He watched her walk down the hall, her lovely hips swaying in that way that was hers alone. Then he took a shower and spent the next few hours staring at the ceiling, watching shadows from the moonlight bounce off the walls through the window. And wondered how he was going to tell Brooke he was in love with her on one hand, and then say he was still leaving on the other.

With that in mind, he figured the best thing to do was to say nothing.

And as much as he was loath to admit it, Matt Laughton shocked the hell out of him over the course of the next couple of days by actually making every effort to be a hands-on, responsible adult with a baby. In between diaper changes, bath time, story time and playtime, he was personable and friendly and appeared to be settling into the role of Cara's father. And the baby seemed accepting enough of the new person in her life. Tyler still made sure he settled her in her crib each night, but he otherwise gave Matt all the space he needed to be able to connect with his daughter. To the other man's credit, he asked for advice when he was in too deep, and accepted feedback with a nod and a smile.

Brooke, on the other hand, avoided him like the plague.

She spent most of her days outside, and in the evenings she spent time with Cara and Matt before turning in to bed early. He convinced himself it was for the best and tried to ignore the ache in his heart and his groin. But he missed her. He missed talking with her. He missed looking into her indigo eyes. He missed the taste of her kiss and the feel of her skin against his. Since that night outside Cara's room she hadn't spared him more than a glance.

"Is my sister giving you the cold shoulder?"

He looked up from his spot at the kitchen table on late Monday afternoon, where he'd been sitting and drinking coffee for the past half hour, and hopeful that Brooke would come through the mudroom so they could talk. But it was Matt in the doorway, looking weary from his last couple of hours entertaining Cara. The baby was in Matt's arms, but she held out her chubby arms when she spotted him and he got up instantly. Matt handed her over, watching as Tyler placed the baby against his chest and patted her back soothingly.

"You make it look easy," Matt said as he moved around the counter to pour himself a mug of coffee.

"It's not easy," Tyler replied. "But you'll get the hang of it with time and effort."

Matt nodded. "You know, you didn't answer the question."

"What question?"

"About what's going on between you and Brooke?"

"Anything that is between your sister and me is going to stay that way."

Matt laughed. "You're even more uptight than she is." And then, more soberly, he asked, "So, have you made a decision? Are you gonna leave Cara here with me?"

Tyler held Cara a little firmer. He knew what he had to do, as much as it pained him. He'd known since that morning when he watched Matt endeavor to soothe Cara as she cried. Matt was trying hard to build a relationship with his daughter and Cara was slowly responding to him. It was what Yelena had wished for and Tyler knew he couldn't stand in the way of that. No matter how much it pained him. "Yes."

Matt nodded, looking relieved, though a little apprehensive. "Thanks."

"It's what Yelena wanted. Just don't screw it up."

"I won't," he promised. "I'll do whatever is best for her, at all times. Not that I planned on being a single parent, but I'll always put her first."

"Good," Tyler said just as Cara started chanting "Dada." He ignored it the best he could, but knew Matt wasn't happy about it and was probably hurt by it. "Anyhow, you've got your sister to help you, so I think you'll be fine."

Matt's expression narrowed slightly and then nodded. "Yeah, about that. She loves Cara a lot. Not that I blame her...but I get why, you know," he said and shrugged loosely, "considering she can't have kids of her own."

Tyler stilled instantly as the other man's words sunk in. "What?"

Matt quickly looked like he wanted to take the words back. "Oh, she didn't tell you. Well, it's not my place to say anything." He was quiet for a moment. "Look, all I'm saying is that it's going to be hard on her, you know, when I go."

"Go?"

"Back to Seattle," he replied. "With Cara."

Tyler's head reeled, first from the bombshell Matt had dropped about Brooke being unable to have a child, and then from his announcement that he was taking Cara away from South Dakota. "You're taking her away from here?"

"I have to," the other man said and shrugged. "I have a life in Seattle, and a home and friends and a business. I can't run a business from here. Unless you're saying I have to stay here in order to get custody of my daughter?"

"No," Tyler said, feeling a heavy weight bear down on his shoulders. "Once legal custody is granted, you can take Cara wherever you want to."

Matt nodded. "Yeah...good. It's just that it's gonna cut Brooke...you know that, right?"

Yes, he knew that. It would break her heart. He also knew there wasn't a damn thing he could do about it.

Chapter Twelve

This is what a broken heart feels like.

Brooke had been nursing one for over twenty-four hours. Ever since Matt had told her the news that Tyler had agreed to grant him custody…and that he was taking Cara back to Seattle. She had an ache inside that couldn't be appeased, and the one thing she wanted she couldn't have—which was Tyler's arms around her. Of course, she couldn't show it. She couldn't let her brother know how unhappy she was. Because she was so conflicted about her feelings. In one way, she was delighted that her brother was grabbing his responsibility with both hands and was determined to be a dad to Cara. But in other ways, she was as unhappy as she could be. Because she'd miss Cara. And because Tyler would be leaving, too.

"Here you are."

Tyler's voice. So familiar. And soon to be so distant. He was leaving with Matt, taking a flight out from Rapid City within hours of her brother. And then she would be alone.

She looked up from her spot in the feed shed. She'd been sitting on a hay bale, hidden from view unless someone took the time to walk around the high stack of bales. Which he'd clearly done. "I'm here. Did you want something?"

"Only to see how you were doing."

"I'm fine," she lied and tried not to think how excruciating it was to exchange pleasantries when all she wanted to do was fall into his arms. "Never better."

"Your aunt called earlier," he commented. "And your friend Kayla. She said you missed a lunch date with her today."

Brooke shrugged. "I'll call and talk to her later."

He moved around the bales and sat down. "So how about you talk to me now."

"I don't feel like it."

He sighed. "Have you tried talking to your brother about how you feel?"

She shrugged again. "Why would I do that? He has to make his own decisions and live his own life. Cara is his child and he has a right to take her with him wherever he goes."

"Of course he does," Tyler said, meeting her gaze steadily. "But considering the circumstances I wonder if he might reconsider his choice and stay here."

Uneasiness wound up her spine. "What circumstances?"

Tyler shifted his feet and then spoke. "That you can't have children."

Heat burned her cheeks as rage and pain surged through her blood. She saw something in Tyler's eyes she had never wanted to see...*pity*. Compassion and pity for the poor barren woman who would never have a child of her own. "My brother, I suppose," she said stiffly. "He had no right to tell you."

"No, he didn't," Tyler agreed. "But I'm glad he did. I understand you a little better now."

"Understand?" she repeated and laughed humorlessly. "You mean you pity me, right? I've seen that look before, Tyler...from my parents and Doyle and even from my friends. So save yourself the trouble of feeling sorry for me. I feel sorry for myself enough."

"I don't feel sorry for you," he said quietly. "But I wish you'd trusted me enough to tell me yourself."

She hurt so much her bones ached. She just wanted him to go away, to take his gentle green-eyed gaze and leave her alone. "Please go away."

"No," he said. "Tell me about it?"

Her mouth flattened. "Tell you about my infertility? What would like to know, Tyler? That I battled endometriosis since I was sixteen or that I've known since I was eighteen that I would never have a child of my own? That I can't create life? That I'm...defective?"

He got to his feet and walked toward her. "Is that really what you think?"

"Yes," she hissed. "It's what I *know*."

"There are other options," he said quietly. "Other ways to—"

"You mean, like surrogacy or adoption?" she said, cutting him off. "Yes, I know all about the options. I've spent over a decade thinking about them or discussing them with well-meaning doctors or friends. But it doesn't change the fact that I can't carry a child of my own. That I can't give..." Her words trailed off painfully. "That I can't give *anyone* a child. So, please, just leave me alone."

"I can't," he admitted hoarsely. "You're hurting."

"So," she said hotly. "I'm hurting. I've hurt before and

I've gotten over it. And I'll get over this. I'll get over never being able to have a child of my own, I'll get over my brother taking Cara away and I'll get over you."

"Do you think that's possible?" he asked and stood directly in front of her. "I don't think I'll ever get you out of my head, Brooke. And frankly, I don't think I want to."

She blinked a couple of times and got to her feet. "What?"

"I don't want to get over you. The truth is, I'm in love with you."

The floor spun and for a second she thought she was going to fall into a heap. "What did you just say?"

"I'm pretty sure you heard me," he said and grabbed her hands. "But, if you must hear it again—I'm in love with you, Brooke."

"But…but you don't believe in love." She threw his words back at him. "You believe in like and lust."

"I believe in love," he said firmly. "Since I met you, I believe in it all."

The pain in her heart increased tenfold. Because she could imagine, for just a moment, that he was handing her the moon and the stars and they were hers to take. But it was a dream. A fantasy. "What do you expect me to say?"

"Well, how about that you feel the same way?"

"What's the point?" she demanded, her heart breaking. She had to give him an out. She didn't want him because he felt sorry for her. "You live in New York. I live here."

"Geography isn't going to cut it as an excuse," he said, rubbing her hands in his, making her melt and making her crazy.

"It's not an excuse, it's a fact. And here's another fact…you want to have a family of your own one day. I know that about you. You told me you want children.

Well, news flash, I can't give them to you. Not now, not ever."

"I don't care about that."

Suddenly it was like Doyle all over again, saying it didn't matter...saying she was enough. When in her heart, she knew she would never be enough. "You will, believe me. Down the track, you'll care. When some random woman shows up on your doorstep with a child she says is yours. Then you'll care. And then you'll run because she can give you what I can't."

She was crying inside, because she was in so much pain, because he didn't realize how much hearing him say he loved her made her love him all the more. But it wasn't enough. Maybe for now, but later, he would want more...he'd deserve more...and it would break her in two knowing she could never give him what he longed for.

She pulled herself from his grasp and stepped back. "Go back to New York, Tyler. Go back to your Manhattan apartment and your hand-stitched suits and before long you'll forget about how you were slumming it in Cedar River for a while."

"Don't say that," he rasped. "Don't cheapen what we have, Brooke, just because you're in pain."

"What we have?" she said, letting out a brittle laugh. "And what's that? One night in bed together. Oh, and of course there was you telling me you didn't want me the other night because I wasn't important."

He scowled. "I didn't say that."

"Sure you did," she snapped. "I practically threw myself at you and you said you wanted to concentrate on what was important...which obviously wasn't me."

"Of course you're important," he said quickly, running a frustrated hand through his hair. "But with your brother coming back and—"

"Oh, spare me," she said, cutting him off. "And none of it matters anyway. Because you live in New York," she reminded him. "And I live *here*. How do you expect to overcome that little complication?"

He shrugged. "I'm not entirely sure."

"That's because you can't. There is no solution in this, Tyler. You can't *fix* this. You've done what you came here to do—you got Cara reunited with her father and you single-handedly saved this place from foreclosure—and now it's time you left."

She pushed past him and raced out of the building. By the time she reached the house she'd calmed herself a little and was wiping the tears off her wet cheeks. She dumped her boots in the mudroom, pushed her feet into loafers and walked into the kitchen. Only to find her brother hovering by the countertop and Cara sitting in her high chair, her little legs bouncing.

"Hey," Matt said and then frowned. "You look like hell."

"Gee…thanks."

He shrugged in his loose-limbed way. "Did Tyler find you? I said you sometimes hang out in the feed shed when you need some thinking time."

She looked at him bitterly. "That's not all you said, is it?"

He looked shamefaced. "It slipped out, Brooke. I'm so sorry. I thought you guys were close." He was quiet for a moment. "I kinda figured you loved the guy."

I do…

So much. But it would never be enough. Maybe he *thought* he was in love with her, but once he was back home the novelty would wear off and he would forget all about her. He had to. He wanted a family. He deserved that. And she could never give it to him. One day he would understand her reasons for pulling away.

"It doesn't matter how I feel."

Matt smiled gently. "You know, it kinda does."

Heat burned her eyes and she blinked. "I can't…" Her words trailed off and she headed for the baby to avoid looking toward her brother. "I can't deny him the family he wants," she said flatly and lifted Cara from the chair. "No matter how I feel."

The back door opened then and Tyler crossed the threshold. Her heart contracted at the sight of him and she blinked hard, fighting back the burn behind her eyes again. Cara squealed delightedly when she saw him and held out her arms, cooing and babbling the word *dada* like she always did when Tyler was around. She noticed the hurt look in Matt's eyes and considered handing him his daughter. But Cara wanted what she wanted—and in that moment she wanted the man who she believed was her daddy.

Tyler took the baby and held her close, his arm brushing Brooke's, and she flinched. He was strong and familiar and she loved him so much, and knowing how much he cared about Cara made her love him even more. And it made her heartsick, too…because she could never give him the children she knew he longed for. She grabbed Cara's hand and the baby clutched her fingers, but the moment was bittersweet. She was losing Cara. And she'd lost Tyler.

She glanced up and saw Matt watching them, looking hurt and confused. She smiled, trying to make the moment somehow easier for her little brother.

"I should pack," Matt said, clearing his throat. "The flight is early in the morning and I have to get to Rapid City."

It was all planned. Tyler would drive Matt and Cara to the airport and then wait for his own flight two hours later. And when they were gone her heart would break in two.

The afternoon dragged on, as did the evening. Brooke spent as much time with the baby as she could, packing her toys and supplies, feeling the grief and loss as she zipped up the bag and placed it by the door along with the rest of Cara's things. By ten Matt was already in bed and Tyler was in the office on his laptop. Brooke hung around the baby's room, watching Cara sleep, trying to absorb as much time with Cara as she could. When she dimmed the night-light she heard a voice from the doorway.

"Hey…are you okay?"

Tyler. She nodded, pushing down the pain she experienced all over. He was watching her, and the look in his eyes had never been more tender. And without a second thought, the truth came out. "I feel like my heart is breaking."

Within seconds he'd pulled her into his arms. "I know, sweetheart," he said soothingly, cradling her head. "I'm so sorry."

Brooke clung to him, feeling his heart thunder in his chest, absorbing his strength into her, finding comfort and solace in his embrace. "Stay with me tonight," she whispered, crumbling. "I need you."

And without another word they walked to her bedroom and closed the door.

They made love slowly, fueled by feelings both said and unsaid. Brooke gave him her heart and body like she'd never given it to anyone before. And he took it, making her mindless, making her love him and making her never want to let him go. But she had to, and at dawn, when he moved over her again and made tender love to every inch of her, she knew what he felt in her touch. He didn't say anything. He didn't have to. They both knew.

It was goodbye.

Leaving Brooke on the porch, watching her figure retreat as he drove the rental car away from the ranch house, was just about the hardest thing Tyler had ever done. Cara was cooing and chatting in the back, oblivious to everything that was going on around her, not knowing she was the catalyst for so much change. Or joy. Or pain.

Beside him, even Matt was unusually quiet. The other man had hugged his sister goodbye for a long time, promising to call when he landed, insisting he'd send photographs and keep Brooke updated on Cara. And Brooke... she looked lost and solitary, alone in her little world. He hadn't told her he loved her again. He couldn't bear to hear the words come from his mouth and then not hear them from her in return. In his heart, he knew she felt them...but she wasn't prepared to give them up, to admit it, to acknowledge that what they had was worth fighting for.

He kissed her softly on the cheek and said he'd be in touch. But he wouldn't. His business in Cedar River was done. He had papers to sign and custody agreements to hand over, but he would do all that through Matt.

And as they drove through the gates and toward town, Tyler felt a sense of loss so acute his heart physically ached. Matt hardly spoke, which suited him just fine, and when they reached the airport he checked in the rental car and grabbed his bag and as many of Cara's things as he could, leaving Matt with the rest. They went through check-in at separate airlines and then Tyler regrouped with Matt by the gate he was leaving from. Cara was on the floor on a play mat and when Tyler sat down she immediately got to her wobbly feet and made it toward him, hanging on to his knee for support. He hauled her into his arms and held her close.

"I think we're all set," Matt said, seeming to be in overly good spirits. If he knew the other man better, Tyler could have sworn he was hanging on by the same thread he was. "How does Cara like flying?"

She giggled at the sound of her name and Tyler held on to her, dreading the moment he knew was coming. When he'd have to give her up. It would be like saying goodbye to Brooke all over again. The baby grabbed a handful of his hair and giggled and he couldn't have loved her more in that moment if she'd been his own child.

"She'll be fine," he assured the other man.

Matt stared at him, then abruptly got to his feet. "I need a minute," he said and walked off, hands on hips, lost in his own thoughts.

Tyler frowned and then nodded. There was something in Matt's expression that concerned him. When the other man returned about twenty minutes later, he had a look of resolve on his face that Tyler hadn't seen before. Not even when he'd first found out about Cara or even when he'd acknowledged that Cara was his own and said he wanted to be a father to her.

"You're in love with my sister, right?" he asked bluntly.

Tyler wasn't about to deny it. "Yes."

Matt nodded. "Brooke loves you, too," he said and sighed heavily. "Even if she can't admit it to you. You know, she's the best person I've ever known—loyal, honest, kind. And she never once laid any blame at my feet for the accident that killed our parents. She could have, I mean, because of me she had to cut short her career, she lost Sky Dancer and then as it turns out she lost her fiancé because she couldn't have kids."

Tyler's insides twitched. "Your point?"

"The point is," Matt said quietly, "is that *you* love her. And *she* loves you."

"She keeps putting obstacles in the way," he admitted wearily, suddenly grateful to be able to say the words to someone who also cared about her.

"Because she can't have kids?" Matt queried. "Does that matter to you?"

"Not at all," he replied, meaning every word. "But she thinks it matters."

Matt shrugged. "She's stubborn. It's unfair the way it worked out for her. I mean, she'd be an awesome mom."

"Yes," Tyler said and swallowed hard. "She would."

Matt let out a long, weary breath and then laughed to himself. "You know, I'm standing here, looking at my daughter and I've just been able to admit to myself one glaringly obvious fact."

Tyler tensed. "And what's that?"

"That she already has a father," Matt said, with a kind of weary resignation. "And that it's not me."

Tyler got to his feet, holding Cara tightly against his chest. "What are you saying?"

"I'm saying that a couple of days ago I told you I would always do what is best for my daughter," Matt said quietly. "And that's exactly what I intend to do."

Before lunch Kayla and Ash stopped by for coffee and commiseration. But she wasn't in the mood. She wanted to flop on her bed, hide her head under the covers and cry for all eternity. But since she couldn't do that because she had a ranch to run, animals needing her attention and a life she had to get back to—post Cara, post Tyler—she invited them inside.

"We're worried about you," Ash said solemnly.

"I'm okay," she assured her friends as they sat around the kitchen table.

"We're pretty sure you're not," Kayla said and smiled gently. "You love him, right?"

She nodded a little. "I guess."

"Does he love you?" Ash asked.

"He said he did."

They both looked surprised. "And he still left?"

"I told him to go," she admitted. "I can't give him what he wants. He wants children of his own and I understand why. And maybe it would be okay now, but one day he'd look back and know he'd settled for less than what he truly wanted. And I love him too much to let him do that. So," she said, taking a deep breath. "It's better this way. Better for everyone."

She made small talk with her friends for an hour and then waved them off after accepting a round of hugs and assurances that everything would work out. *Sure it will*, she thought as she waved them off.

I just need to grow a new heart...

Brooke tidied up the house for a while, finding things everywhere that reminded her of the baby. By the time she made it to her own room her eyes were stinging, and suddenly faced with the crumpled duvet on her bed only amplified her loneliness. She sat on the edge of the bed and remembered every moment she'd spent with Tyler between the sheets. Not nearly long enough, her heart sang out. But she had memories she would cherish and his tender touch was forever imprinted on her skin and in her heart. No man had ever come close to making her feel what she had felt with him. And no man, she suspected, ever would.

She heard the dogs barking outside and ignored them. All she wanted to do was sleep. And dammit, *dwell*.

But she didn't. She straightened her back and headed for the guest room, where she stripped the bed and tidied up a little before tossing the sheets in the laundry hamper. Then she went to Cara's room. It looked just like it had before Cara and Tyler had entered her life. The desk, her mom's old sewing machine, a chest filled with old family memorabilia in one corner. Only the baby monitor sitting on the desk was out of place. She was sure she'd packed it with the rest of Cara's things. Or perhaps she'd left it behind deliberately. Brooke grabbed the monitor and flicked it on. Waiting for a sound. But nothing came. She grabbed it and popped it in a small box with a few stray toys and a little pink coat that had been stranded in the washing machine and placed the box on the kitchen table.

With a wistful sigh she filled the kettle to make tea and opened the refrigerator, scouring the contents for something to eat. She ended up in the pantry and chose a noodle cup. The dogs were still yapping and she was just about to head out through the mudroom and call them to heel when she heard a faint crackling sound. She stopped, rooted to her spot by the door. And listened. More crackling. And a low screech. Coming from the box on the table. And then a word.

Dada...

She shook her head. Impossible. Her mind was playing a cruel trick. She made her way over to the table and peered into the box. Lights were flashing on the monitor. And more indecipherable words came through.

Brooke's legs almost gave way and she clutched the table for support. How could this be?

I'm hallucinating...

She inhaled a long breath, felt strength seep into her blood and then straightened her back.

I can do this. I have to do this.

She walked up the hallway, and when she reached the front door her hands were shaking so much she could barely turn the knob. She opened the door and swung it back on its hinges.

Tyler stood on the porch, Cara happily gurgling in his arms, the baby monitor in his hand.

She stayed where she was, confused and overwhelmed.

"So, no shotgun this time," he said, smiling. "That's a step in the right direction."

"What are you doing here?"

His mouth twisted slightly. "Can we come inside?"

Cara was making a whole bunch of squealing noises and the volume amplified when Brooke opened the screen door and Tyler crossed the threshold.

"I don't understand," she said, still in shock, staring at the man and baby now in her hallway. "What…what… I think I must be dreaming."

"You're not dreaming," he assured her. "Can we go into the living room so I can put her down?"

They moved up the hall and Brooke was sure her knees were knocking together. Tyler placed Cara on the carpet by the sofa and then withdrew an envelope from the inside of his jacket.

"For you," he said quietly. "From Matt."

Brooke stared at the envelope and then met Tyler's gaze unsteadily. She swallowed the lump in her throat and took the envelope with shaking fingers. Once she was sitting she withdrew a note from inside and recognized her brother's scrawl.

Brooke
I know you're gonna think I'm crazy, or maybe you won't. I've been doing a lot of thinking and know that I have to do what's right for Cara. I owe Yelena

that, at least. But you know, that's the damnable thing about doing what's right, sometimes there's no way to stop someone getting hurt. So, I figure the only way for the least amount of people to get hurt is to do what I'm doing.

You asked me if I'd made peace with the accident... but I don't think I have. I'm still running. And I don't want to take my kid on the run, if you get my meaning. I know I could probably do a good job at raising her, but she deserves more than that. She deserves what I saw the other day when we were all in the kitchen...the three of you together, like a real family. That's what we had growing up and I want my kid to have that, too.

Don't think this isn't the hardest thing I'm ever gonna do, because I know it is. But I know it's the right thing and I hope one day Cara will know that, too.

I love you, sis. And I promise to keep in touch.

Matt x

Brooke read the words again and then folded the note over. She met Tyler's level gaze. He was standing by the fireplace, one hand on the mantel. "What does this mean?"

"Your brother is giving up his parental rights. To you. To us both."

Her heart leaped in her chest. "But... I don't understand? Did you see this coming and—"

"No," he replied, cutting her off. "I didn't see it coming. I'm pretty sure Matt didn't, either, until we were at the airport."

The note trembled in her shaking hand. "I should be happy about this. But I think I'm terrified. And in shock."

"Yeah," he said and grinned fractionally. "I was like that on the drive home."

Home...

Her insides were jumping in time with her knocking knees. "What does this really mean, Tyler?" she asked again.

"From a legal point of view," he said, coming around the sofa, "it means that your brother is giving us joint custody." He sat down, barely a foot away from her. "From a you-and-me point of view... I guess that really depends on you."

"On me?" She shook her head.

"Sure," he said and was suddenly on the floor in front of her, on his haunches. He grabbed her hands and the note crumpled between them. "It depends on how you feel. It depends on whether or not you'll marry me."

Marry him?

Brooke took a deep breath to stop herself from hyperventilating. "You want to marry me?"

"I want to marry you," he said and moved closer, "more than I've ever wanted anything in my life."

She couldn't move. Couldn't breathe. "But why, Tyler? For Cara's sake?"

"No," he said gently and rubbed the bare ring finger on her left hand with his thumb. "I want to marry you because I'm completely in love with you. And Cara," he said and grinned as the baby came wobbling toward them and grabbed on to Brooke's knees. "She's a bonus. An adorable bonus, just the same. But if there was no Cara," he said, gripping her hand tightly. "If there was just you and me, I would still want to marry you. I would still love you."

Brooke reached out and touched his face. "But...how can we? I live here and you live in New York and—"

He silenced her by placing two fingers against her lips. "Do you know what this town needs?" he said and grinned. "It needs a good lawyer."

Brooke's breath caught in her throat. "Are you saying…"

"I'm saying that I want to be where you are."

"But you told me you were up for partnership soon and you've worked hard for that and I can't—"

"The only partnership I'm interested in," he said, cutting her off again, "is this one. The one where we raise Cara together, as husband and wife."

It was all happening so fast. "You'd give everything up…for me…for this?"

"Absolutely."

Love for him coursed through her blood and over her skin. "But, Tyler…you know what that means? Your career isn't the only thing you'll have to give up." She blinked back the tears in her eyes. "I can never give you a child."

He looked at Cara and smiled lovingly. "We have a child."

It was a lovely dream. But she had to be sure. "I mean a child of your own. I've accepted that I can't have children, but it's unfair of me to expect someone else to accept that, too. Can you give up the dream of having a child that shares your blood and your genes and your—"

"Brooke," he said, a little firmer as he grasped her chin and leveled their gazes. "I was adopted. Do you think it matters to me how we become a family?"

"But you divorced your parents and—"

"Not because I resented them or didn't think of them as my real parents," he explained softly. "I was young and ambitious and arrogant and I didn't want to live the life they had. But I love them dearly. I know I hurt them badly when I filed for emancipation and I can only try to make up for that by being the best kind of man I can, the man they raised me to be. They're my parents and I know they love me and would do anything for me. And they're going to love you, too," he assured her. "And Cara."

Love surged in her heart, but resistance lingered. "Are you sure?"

"Never surer," he said and kissed her.

"This has all happened so fast I can barely catch my breath."

"It has been fast," he agreed. "And you have done your fair share of making me breathless. But I'm not going to second-guess how I feel about you, Brooke. I fell in love with you here, in this room," he said and glanced around. "And in the kitchen and the stables and on the porch and in your bed. I fell in love with your kindness and your honesty and your beautiful indigo eyes. You're the last person I want to see before I fall asleep at night. And the first person I want to see when I wake up. Now," he said against her mouth. "Is there something you'd like to tell me?"

Brooke smiled, so happy she could barely believe it. "Oh, yes... I will marry you."

His eyes glittered. "That wasn't exactly what I meant, but it will do."

She smiled again as Cara started calling him "Dada" and began climbing all over him. "Oh...the other thing," she teased and reached out to touch his face lovingly. "I love you."

He sighed and smiled a little. "You took your time."

"But was it worth it?"

He kissed her sweetly. "You bet."

"And from now on I'll tell you every day."

"Or I'll remind you to tell me," he said and scooped Cara into his arms.

"You won't need to," she said and laughed happily.

And sure enough, he didn't.

Epilogue

"You're not going outside unless you get blindfolded."

Brooke stood her ground. "I am not wearing a blind-fold. And I don't like surprises."

They'd been having the same conversation for the past ten minutes. He was by the bedroom door, blocking her exit. Tyler had a surprise for her and she had to wear a bandanna tied around her eyes. Not going to happen.

"Stop being a spoilsport."

"Stop being bossy," she snapped back. "And where's Cara?"

"In her crib playing. She's perfectly happy and safe. Now," he said and held up a blue bandanna. "Put this on."

"No."

He laughed and her temper at his high-handedness disappeared. He could turn her to mush with just a look. And he knew it. "Can't I keep my eyes tightly shut? It's the same thing."

"You'll peek."

"I will not!" she denied indignantly. "I'm not a peeker."

"Sure you are." He laughed again and the sound rumbled in his chest so deliciously she felt her desire for him overshadow her irritation at him for waking her up on a Sunday morning and then announcing he had a surprise for her.

His last surprise had been a doozy—he'd bought out Werner Stewart's law practice and her old lawyer had decided to retire and vacation in Florida for the unforeseeable future. She and Tyler had been married ten days ago in a civil ceremony and had a small reception at the Parker Ranch, after a whirlwind engagement that lasted just over a month. Before the wedding, Tyler had returned to New York briefly, to resign and hand over his caseload and to turn down an offer for a partnership. He'd come back with his personal belongings and Mr. Squiggles, the fluffy cat who had once belonged to Yelena and who now spent his day terrorizing the dogs. But she knew Tyler had no regrets. They had a life to build together with Cara, and now that the ranch was financially stable and Tyler had his new law practice, she had never been happier.

"Okay," she said and crawled out of bed. "I give in."

Tyler met her by the foot of the bed and dangled the bandanna. "Ready?"

She nodded. "Just don't let me bang into anything."

He chuckled and gently tied the cloth around her eyes. "I promise to protect you with my life."

Her heart rolled lovingly. Because she knew he would. He was a wonderful husband and such an amazing father to Cara that every time she saw him with the baby she fell in love with him a little bit more. And Cara was flourishing. She was walking and talking and always happy. The adoption process was in motion and it wouldn't be long before they would legally be able to call her their daughter.

She'd heard from Matt and although she knew her brother was hurting, she also believed he was at peace with his decision. He called her regularly, a far cry from the impersonal texts she'd been getting for the past five years. He always asked after Cara, but never referred to the baby as his daughter.

"What about Cara?" she asked as he opened the door and led her through.

"I'll get her," he said and steadied her as they walked down the hall. "Stay here. And no peeking."

Brooke laughed and soon he was back by her side, with Cara in one arm. He led her down the hallway and toward the front door. Anticipation rose up and she started smiling as he opened the front door and security screen. The dogs were on the porch, bouncing around, and Tyler gave them the command to heel.

"Okay," he said and touched the bandanna. "Ready?"

Brooke nodded. "Yep."

He removed the cloth and she blinked a few times to get her bearings in the morning sunlight. She spotted her cousin Grady's truck and horse trailer parked by the stables immediately.

"What's this?" she queried.

"Go take a look," he said and grinned.

Brooke was down the steps in a flash and heading across the yard. Grady was at the back of the trailer and by the time she reached him he had the tailgate down and was back inside the trailer. Brooke heard the pound of hooves and a breathless snort as a huge, dark chestnut horse with a flaxen mane and tail was led backward down the ramp.

The moment she realized what was actually happening, Brooke's eyes almost popped out of their sockets. She would recognize the powerful colt anywhere.

Cloud Dancer...

Grady was smiling as he led the horse into the corral, released him and then shut the gate.

"It's good to see things getting back to how they were around here," Grady said as he gave her an affectionate hug. He waved hello to Tyler, who was now walking toward the corral, and then headed back to his truck. He locked up the tailgate and drove off without saying another word. Brooke stood by the corral, watching, captivated as the beautiful colt pranced around the yard, tail up, head held at a proud, regal angle.

"Happy?"

Tyler's voice dragged her from her horse trance. She turned, tears flowing. "I can't believe you did this."

He shrugged loosely, but he looked pleased. "He sure is something."

"How?" she asked, grasping Tyler's strong arm. "How did you do this?"

"Grady helped," he supplied. "It wasn't hard to track him down. Negotiating with his previous owner wasn't easy, but he eventually came around."

"I know how much he would have cost," she said and shook her head, "It's way too generous."

"Nothing is too much for you," he said gently. "I wanted to do this, so you can rebuild this place. So you can continue your parents' legacy. So you can have everything you've ever dreamed of."

"Thank you," Brooke said as she smiled and pressed close to him. Cara grabbed her hand and chuckled as she rested her head against Tyler's chest. "But I already have everything I've dreamed of, right here."

And she did. Her family. Their family. Forever.

* * * * *

Don't miss the previous books in Helen Lacey's
new series, **THE CEDAR RIVER COWBOYS:**
THREE REASONS TO WED
and
LUCY & THE LIEUTENANT

MILLS & BOON®

Cherish™

EXPERIENCE THE ULTIMATE RUSH OF FALLING IN LOVE

A sneak peek at next month's titles...

In stores from 8th September 2016:

- **A Mistletoe Kiss with the Boss** – Susan Meier *and* **Maverick vs Maverick** – Shirley Jump
- **A Countess for Christmas** – Christy McKellen *and* **Ms Bravo and the Boss** – Christine Rimmer

In stores from 6th October 2016:

- **Her Festive Baby Bombshell** – Jennifer Faye *and* **Building the Perfect Daddy** – Brenda Harlen
- **The Unexpected Holiday Gift** – Sophie Pembroke *and* **The Man She Should Have Married** – Patricia Kay

Just can't wait?
Buy our books online a month before they hit the shops!
www.millsandboon.co.uk

Also available as eBooks.

MILLS & BOON®

EXCLUSIVE EXCERPT

Emma Carmichael's world is turned upside-down
when she encounters Jack Westwood—her
secret husband of six years!

Read on for a sneak preview of
A COUNTESS FOR CHRISTMAS
the first book in the enchanting new Cherish quartet
MAIDS UNDER THE MISTLETOE

'You still have your ring,' Jack said.

'Of course.' Emma was frowning now and wouldn't
meet his eye.

'Why—?' He walked to where she was standing
with her hand gripping her handbag so hard her
knuckles were white.

'I'm not very good at letting go of the past,' she
said, shrugging and tilting up her chin to look him
straight in the eye, as if to dare him to challenge her
about it. 'I don't have a lot left from my old life and
I couldn't bear to get rid of this ring. It reminds me of
a happier time in my life. A simpler time, which I don't
want to forget about.'

She blinked hard and clenched her jaw together
and it suddenly occurred to him that she was strug-
gling with being around him as much as he was with
her.

The atmosphere hung heavy and tense between them,

with only the sound of their breathing breaking the silence.

His throat felt tight with tension and his pulse had picked up so he felt the heavy beat of it in his chest.

Why was it so important to him that she hadn't completely eschewed their past?

He didn't know, but it was.

Taking a step towards her, he slid his fingers under the thin silver chain around her neck, feeling the heat of her soft skin as he brushed the backs of his fingers over it, and drew the ring out of her dress again to look at it.

He remembered picking this out with her. They'd been so happy then, so full of excitement and love for each other.

He heard her ragged intake of breath as the chain slid against the back of her neck and looked up to see confusion in her eyes, and something else. Regret, perhaps, or sorrow for what they'd lost.

Something seemed to be tugging hard inside him, drawing him closer to her.

Her lips parted and he found he couldn't drag his gaze away from her mouth. That beautiful, sensual mouth that used to haunt his dreams all those years ago.

A lifetime ago.

Don't miss
A COUNTESS FOR CHRISTMAS
by Christy McKellen

Available October 2016

www.millsandboon.co.uk